The Lady of McCalleys Creek

A Lowcountry Shrimping & Crabbing Adventure

Terry L. Futrell

Based on True Events

WAYWORD
ADVENTURES

Contact the author at www.waywordadventures.com

Publisher's Cataloging-in-Publication Data
Names: Futrell, Terry L., author.
Title: The lady of McCalleys Creek: a lowcountry shrimping and crabbing adventure / Terry L. Futrell.
Description: Murfreesboro, NC: Terry L. Futrell, 2024.
Identifiers: ISBN 978-1-966219-00-2 (paperback) | ISBN 978-1-966219-01-9 (hardcover) | ISBN 978-1-966219-02-6 (ebook)
Subjects: LCSH: Women fishers--South Carolina--Biography. | Shrimpers (Persons)--South Carolina--Biography. | South Carolina--Social life and customs. | Ghosts--South Carolina. | Providence and government of God--Christianity.. | Autobiography. | BISAC: BIOGRAPHY & AUTOBIOGRAPHY / Memoirs. | BIOGRAPHY & AUTOBIOGRAPHY / Women.
Classification: LCC PS3606.U87 L69 2024 (print) | LCC PS3606.U87 (ebook) | DDC 814/.092
--dc23.

LCCN: 2024924379

WayWORD Adventures, LLC
Murfreesboro, NC

Dedicated to Lindsey,

my beautiful daughter

Table of Contents

Introduction

Feet hit the floor very early during crab and shrimp season. Fog rolls over the water's edge like an ominous scene in a horror film. They say time and tide wait for no man. I think we shall rewrite that to say "time and tide wait for neither man nor woman" to be more correct. However, in this modern world we live in today, maybe we just say, the tide waits for no one.

Boats enter the water to be in position for the tide. The tide rises and falls eight to ten feet every six hours around here in the South Carolina Lowcountry.

One of the first things a doctor friend told me was, when you hit a sandbar, not if, but when you do, sit back, open a beer, grab a snack, listen to the music and relax. It will only be six hours until you're floating again and you can go home. It's a way of life in the Lowcountry: high tide, low tide and the highest tide of all, the King Tide. Muddy ditches one minute, then flourishing streams the next, all because of the ever-changing tide.

Local fishermen told me inshore shrimping on a smaller day boat is the ideal way to get into the seafood arena in the Lowcountry. So that's what I did; I went out and found a twenty-five-foot shrimper. Then, I thought, just as well get into crabbing to complete this fishing adventure.

Never did understand the logic of taking small steps.

After some research online, I discovered a twenty-two-foot boat with a 150 Yamaha and an electric puller would handle the job nicely. So, I bought a local boat, motor and trailer from a fellow crabber of many years.

Couldn't hurt to have an experienced boat, right?

If only that boat could tell the stories of its time on these waters as it chased crab pots up and down these muddy ditches and throughout the intercoastal waterway. These two boats should do nicely, I thought. Let's face it, any reason to buy a new boat is a good reason, and it really only takes one.

Position is everything on these waters. Where your pots float becomes your real estate, and the first man to drag at high tide is certain to fill his nets, the locals say. So, the race to pull your net first was always the challenge. Locals said to start with one hundred pots and see how it goes out there. Never know about this crowd; they're tough. The local crabbers think they own these waters here. I wasn't concerned. I ordered my pots, got a specific color, length of rope and floats, just as I wanted.

Crabbing and shrimping in this town can be a hard way of life, sometimes described as a violent and vicious way to make a living. It can take a person's livelihood to a whole different level. No rule these crabbers wouldn't break. No laws to protect you or governing bodies that are capable of patrolling and enforcing regulations on this massive amount of water.

Pots float only as long as man's greed lets them. It was open season on unwanted crabbers and shrimpers. Instead of a "Visitors Welcome" sign when entering town, it should read "New Crabbers and Shrimpers Not Welcome." With all that said, let's hit the water and pull a few pots and drag a net!

I can tell you, parking a crab boat or shrimp boat is not as easy as it would seem. Having your own dock is a must or at least makes it easier. Working boats are a little messy from time to time. Not what you want parked beside your fancy restaurant. My shrimp boat, which I called my Little Drag-in Wagon, was pretty, but you had to work at keeping her that way.

Better to have a good GPS and depth finder on the boats, that's for sure. With the tide rising and falling every six hours, things looked different from one hour to the next, all day and throughout the night. The depth finder would certainly save you from running aground and beaching on one of the many sandbars.

Now, white boots and bibs were a must as well. Got to look the part, you know. Mine fit rather well, I thought. A whole lot different from the scrubs and lab coats I'm accustomed to wearing.

Let's buy a house on the water. Can't be too hard to find, right? All this water around here. Wrong – not easy. Well, perhaps I got lucky. Good luck or bad luck, you decide, as I tell this story.

Chapter 1

Good Memories

I was once told when we leave this Earth, we only carry our memories with us, so we better make some good ones.

These waters certainly provided plenty of those, good and bad. Life on the water in a thriving tourist community sounded like a dream come true. It was, in the beginning. Get in, get situated and retire – sounded like a great plan. With all this water, boating on some level would be logical.

Now, you know what they say about a boat. The first day you buy it is a happy day, but the day you sell it is really one of the happiest days of your life. That is so true, my friend. Don't get me wrong, spending a day on the water is more wonderful than any day spent indoors, that's for sure.

To say the landscape in the Lowcountry is beautiful wouldn't do it justice. The landscape in the Lowcountry has beauty of which can only be described as stunning and breathtaking; and it can only really be appreciated when witnessed firsthand. The moss twisting and turning, blowing in the breeze, as it hangs on the limbs of the great angel oaks, creating a mysterious, yet elegant scene. The sun, the warm water, the sea gulls, pelicans and dolphins create a spectacular atmosphere with an occasional turtle popping its head up to say "Hi." All God's creation, a gift of beauty and grace. Life rolled in and out with each tide.

Overwhelming at times, the pleasure and peace this backdrop provided. Coming from a life in my professional career of cold, dark, sterile fields, this was a wonderful change and an experience I was glad I had. Warm sunlight on my face, watching the sun rise from out deep in the marsh. Beautiful colors reflecting over the water. Heaven on earth.

I kept my camera strapped to my bibs, so I was ready at all times. I didn't want to miss that perfect picture. Each morning was another opportunity to capture that once-in-a-lifetime sunrise. As I sent pictures of my days on the water to family, friends and coworkers, I described it as my new office. A total life change, an unimaginable transformation.

They enjoyed these beautiful views just as much as I did. Looking back, I see God let me experience all these spectacular wonders, and in time, God delivered me out of this nightmare. Nothing can take this chapter of my life away from me; I cannot forget it, nor do I want to. I do remember and reflect on the good and thank God for saving me to experience what next adventures He has in store.

Chapter 2

Little Drag-in Wagon

My Little Drag-in Wagon, a powerful pulling machine. She's a twenty-five-foot Louisiana skiff with a 210 Cummins diesel, pulling a thirty-five-foot shrimp net with a Texas rigging. "A day boat," they said. "That's what you need." So that's what I got. "Get your boat and get ready. This year is going to be golden. This will be the year we've been waiting for and needing. Shrimp are going to be early this year and plentiful." The waters are already warming up.

All signs point to a spectacular year. I found my day boat – my little shrimper – and brought her home on a borrowed trailer. Cleaned her up, gave her a fresh coat of paint, made a few adjustments to the support beams and my little shrimper and I were on our way. Having vast knowledge of the North Carolina waters and being new to the South Carolina waters, I felt more comfortable hiring a local captain. Now was the time to start looking for this individual.

The Lowcountry has a rich history of shrimping with family lines of shrimpers and watermen in general, going back through time, generation after generation.

Well, as it goes, the owner of the borrowed trailer needed it back sooner than later; basically, right now.

As other times throughout my life when I needed help and guidance, God has shown favor upon me and covered my needs. Now this day, God showed up again with the perfect solution for the crisis at hand. I had to either find another trailer or find a dock to park my little shrimper.

I have been told throughout my life, talking to every-one and anyone is a gift I got from my Grandpop the "gift of gab," as they say back home. One day I was talking at work, on my real job – as it so happened during an MRI study with an anesthesiologist – about my little shrimper. The anesthesiologist in this case happened to have owned a wedding venue with a very nice pier at the local neighborhood ramp. He said I could dock there for a short time. Wow, I was excited! What an honor. No one had ever been invited to park there before, according to local gossip. The real questions the locals had were, "Who does she think she is? Who is she?"

Doesn't hurt to be friendly and talk to everyone; you never know who God has put in your path. Some are blessings to help you or advance your soul and purpose and some are to cause detours on this road of life. I saw this doctor with his beautiful barn and dock as a blessing. Driving over the bridge, you could see the wildlife boat ramp, the wedding barn and its dock. What a relief for my little shrimper to be securely docked for the moment.

Royal blue and white, she was – "cute as a speckle puppy sitting in a red wagon," as they would say back in North Carolina.

Well, now we were in the water, and I couldn't wait to take her for a spin. The neighbor down the street was a captain. He was known in these parts as Captain Bob. He was experienced in the waters here, chartering fishing trips from time to time, both inshore and throughout the intercoastal waterway. We got together on schedules and planned a short trip to see how the little shrimper would handle out on these waters. It was a great trip; we familiarized ourselves with the boat and its equipment and got a feel for how it handled.

Bob and I both were extremely excited and now ready to go drag the bottom of these waterways for the iconic and precious Lowcountry shrimp. It would soon be shrimping season for little boats like mine. Inshore shrimpers are what we're called. I could hardly wait to go drag and neither could Bob.

The day came that Captain Bob and I, along with Ben – a close friend of Bob's – took to the seas to try our hand at shrimping. A three-hour tour of sorts, as they would say on a TV show from my childhood. We headed out early that morning because it would take some time to get out to the five-mile marker where it was legal to drag nets for shrimp on boats my size. Three or four hours to get out and just as many to get back. You see, my boat is made for pulling, not for speed.

As I mentioned before, sandbars are plentiful here, and wouldn't you know it, I hit one going out that morning. Bob was on it, though. He quickly took the wheel, put her in reverse and backed us right off that sandbar. I was extremely proud of him as I watched him maneuver my vessel.

Once we were off the sandbar, he returned the wheel to me, and we continued along our course to the area where we planned to drag. The water was a little choppy that morning, but would hopefully calm down sooner or later, or at least before we reached the drag field. The farther out we traveled, the rougher the water seemed to get. Our boat was handling and maneuvering well, so we continued.

As we traveled along, laughing, joking, and enjoying the sun, we relaxed, let our hair down and turned the music up. At one point I felt honored; I was gifted with a front row seat to a concert. The Drag-in Wagon had quite a stereo system. Bob and Ben, enjoying the music, took to the back deck, performing to each song that came on the radio. What a show – these boys could sing and dance. Swinging from the support beams, busting out dance moves, singing word for word to each song. Good times, good memories, and good friends make for good days. We had a long ride, so this surely helped pass the time. Laughter is good for the spirit and soul. As I listened to the music, it reminded me of another time in my life.

My thoughts reflected all the way back to the first boat I bought as an adult. It was an eighteen-foot red and silver metal-flake ski boat with a 150 Johnson mounted on the back. Supposedly, you can fish off anything if you have the desire, hold your mouth right and the moon's phase graciously shows favor upon you.

I mounted a trolling motor to the bow and she was fish ready. Now, she didn't have a radio, just an eight-track tape player and they were outdated years before I bought the boat. So, no one had any eight-track tapes. We were stuck playing the one that came with the boat. "Cocaine" was the song; we traveled up and down the Chowan River with that one song blasting loudly over the speakers.

The shrimper was equipped to play almost anything and even had a loudspeaker. Another hour into our voyage and still bigger waves. We all realized at the same time the situation had changed. Now it was not looking as if the water would calm down at this point.

"What do you think, Captain?" I asked.

"Not looking good," Bob replied.

Once we were there, we decided it was a no-go at that time. So, we didn't drop the net. This day would not be the day we had hoped for and anxiously awaited. How very disappointing. Well, let's turn around and head back.

By now the waves were about seven feet high and breaking over the bow. "Back it up, Terry. Put it in reverse, Terry," the phrase from a popular, viral YouTube video, took on a whole new meaning for us. I was thinking at that point we could possibly capsize or unwillingly go swimming on some unwanted level. Either way we were about to get wet.

At this moment, my thoughts took me back to a time when I was younger. I was on a family fishing trip with my father, mother, sister and little brother and the family pet, Skipper. Skipper was a mountain terrier, loved by the entire family. We had her for many years. Skipper tagged along everywhere we went, most of the time in the back window of the family car. Well, today she was our fishing companion. A beautiful day on the water; the fish weren't biting but it was a pretty day, nonetheless.

Today a discussion of dogs swimming and how they all automatically know how, happened to arise. So, our father thought he would show us. He threw Skipper off the boat and right into the water. Wouldn't you know it, she had no idea how to swim. Up and then down under the surface, then up again and down once more. This continued for a minute, down, up, down, up and then down again. You get the point.

"Daddy, Daddy, do something!" my sister yelled loudly. She continued yelling, "Somebody get the net!"

Daddy took the net and scooped Skipper up. Pulled her back into the boat and you could tell she was relieved. So no, all dogs cannot swim. Just so you know.

Waves continued to crash over the bow and sea spray was now blowing across the deck. As each wave would rise and fall, it would twist the backend of the boat around. Whitecaps were plentiful and the oceans spray was hitting the windshield, wipers running on high-speed, moving the water so I could see.

Thankfully, they were working as they should. Definitely an advantage in this situation. I looked over my shoulder at the beacon mounted on the cabin wall. What a big comfort it was knowing if we were to go down, the water hitting the beacon would trigger an alarm, sending out a signal to the Coast Guard we were in the water and needed help.

A good friend and a local boat builder once told me, if

you are ever out on the water and start to go down or even think you might go down, grab a life vest, get it on and find the beacon. Strap the beacon to your arm and keep it tight to your body. If you end up in the water, the Coast Guard will pick you up soon. I had just purchased the beacon the day before from a local boat store. I wasn't going to buy it at first, but my sister adamantly insisted that I do and so I did. Thank goodness she had the foresight to see what could happen. I returned to the store, purchased the beacon and went home. A few hours after I bought it, she called to make sure the beacon would be on the boat for this trip to the five-mile marker. My sister called often to check on me and hear of any new adventures. She loves me dearly and was obviously worried about my safety.

As I turned the boat around, I stayed high on the roll of the waves, watching closely to gauge each wave as I handled my vessel to secure the safety of the crew and myself. Minutes felt like hours at this point. A stressful time for sure. But man, I sure felt alive. My adrenaline level was off the chart, my heart was pounding rapidly, and I was breathing fast enough for one breath to push the next out of the way. If there was ever a time to pray, now was the time.

My mom once told me, "If your knees are shaking, fall on them and pray." A wise, soft-spoken, warm-hearted woman, admired by all who know her. She has always had a way to influence me with little sayings that are easy for me to remember. Sayings that have been proven through time to offer encouragement, comfort and support.

I took this time to pray to God, asking Him to place His hands on us and my boat, guiding us to calmer waters, while keeping us safe and dry. As the sky cleared in the distance, a *rainbow* appeared. This was a sign for me; I had not ridden these waves alone. My little brother Roy and Daddy were with me. A rainbow has appeared for me from time to time since their passing whenever difficult times present themselves. This is a common sign seen by my mother and sister as well.

Slowly we continued back on the same path we had traveled on just hours before. That's where the GPS comes in handy. The same one that will keep you off the sandbars, if you're watching. A lesson learned without harm was a good lesson.

We eventually made it back to the dock after a few hours, all safe and dry. I was so relieved and quite frankly thankful to my crew for accompanying me on that spectacular journey. I could tell by the looks on their faces they felt a great sense of accomplishment as well. Whoa, did we just do that? Took the Little Drag-in Wagon out to the five-mile marker. It was a trip I'll never forget and an experience not many can say they have ever had. Bragging rights, that's for sure. No shrimp caught but memories, great memories – the kind I shall reflect upon for the rest of my days. And memories like these are worthy to take with us beyond, as I was once told by a friend.

As a commercial fisherman or a boat owner in general, there's a call you never want to get. "The boat is taking-on water. She's sinking at the dock," the caller said. His voice was shaking and he was breathing rapidly. "I just came over the bridge and saw her myself."

"I'm on the way," I said. As I jumped in my truck, one thought came to my mind. I don't have any insurance on her yet. Could this really be happening? Could I lose her at the dock? Having a commercial fishing boat is stressful, but this crisis took things to a whole different level.

I tend to drive a little fast on my normal daily routes, but this threat had my blood pressure elevated just a little higher, so I was traveling faster than normal. Quickly, I thought of my friends who lived close to the landing. I called them both, told them my situation and they just happened to be working on their properties. They grabbed their cohorts, their portable pumpers and were at the dock just a few steps behind me. My other friend, a boat builder, lived down that way as well. He heard the distress call and met me at the dock also. Together, with all the locals helping, we pumped the water out, lifting her back up to a normal level and started figuring out what happened to cause this threat. My boat builder friend said I needed larger bilge pumps – pumps capable of pumping large amounts of water out quickly in any event water comes over the bow or into the boat in general, when out on the water or sitting at the dock, basically sinking for any reason. These pumps can save your life in these events. Heavy rainfall brought this situation to our attention. That day my friends and their mobile bilge pumps saved my little shrimper on the dock. An eye-opening experience, that's for sure. How sad that would have been to lose my boat that early in the game.

With the situation under control, my fellow watermen and friends disbursed, going back to their daily routines. Thanking them all for their assistance and quick response time was the least I could do. I felt honored to have such great people to call my friends here. I felt like a part of the fishing community. Boater to boater and fisherman to fisherman, a member of a group that was so new to me.

What comradery exists amongst this water community? A great bond between neighbors and fellow boaters. The waterman's oath: "Never leave a fellow boater." They hold this maritime rule close to their hearts with utmost respect and importance.

Now it was time to move the boat; there was a wedding planned this weekend at the barn, according to my doctor friend. The time spent here had served its purpose. I refueled the boat, cleaned her up and looked for a new dock for her to park.

I located a new dock and now needed a captain and crew to accompany me with the move. I found and hired a few good people to help and off we went.

"She's a sharp boat," the crew boasted. "She handles well, engine runs smooth, strong and steady." They were pleased and impressed with the little shrimper. I was very happy with her myself and proud she was mine. The journey to the new dock would be a pleasant and exciting experience for me. The route would take us through new territories, areas on these waters I had not yet explored. Along the way, we encountered beautiful views of the shoreline and an occasional island with beautiful white sandy beaches. The coastline still showed evidence of recent storms, even remains from a devastating hurricane. From time to time a cottage would appear, and as we passed, I wondered what it must be like to wake up in the mornings and look out across this water, seeing the sunrise and all the beauty that surely one would experience here. I was so excited for the owners.

As my Big Ma taught me when I was young, God blesses good people with good gifts and heavenly favor. I can imagine her saying those owners are surely blessed by the grace of God. She was a small lady with a big heart and a strong faith in God. She passed away when I was young, so I don't have many memories of her, but the few I have I treasure.

Finally, we made it to the new dock. As we approached, I was taken by surprise at the view. What a beautiful sight! Larger shrimp boats were parked along the docks, one after the other. I never knew there were so many working shrimp boats still in the area. Definitely a great opportunity to capture some wonderful pictures. This was a pleasant surprise. I was happy the owner of the dock allowed me to park there, but this was overwhelming. My boat was so much smaller than the others. These were big boys, big shrimpers, the real deal.

I felt like a pony in the big horse barn.

We docked the boat, secured the lines, locked the cabin and headed home. Another wonderful day on the water here in the Lowcountry.

Days after arriving at our new dock, a gentleman approached me inquiring about the opportunity to captain my boat. "Tony's my name, ma'am, Tony." He was a polite young man, strong and eager to work. He was from a long line of shrimpers, shrimping these waters generation after generation. He possessed unlimited knowledge of nets, their riggings and shrimping techniques, unmatched by new generations today. Tony's family had acquired this knowledge by working for many years aboard the older shrimpers. Techniques learned through time and experience aboard these boats as they would drag up and down the waters here in the Lowcountry. Dragging deep waters, shallow waters and along the shoreline or the banks edge would all require different techniques. Knowing when to drag and when to sit on the porch would also be a lesson to learn. Tony's grandfather, father and uncles passed along this information, as they worked side by side to provide for their families. As a matter of fact, back in the day, many years ago this very dock had belonged to his great-grandmother. Tony was actually kin to the group of young men I had hired to move the boat from the doctor's barn to the new dock as well.

We sat on the boat talking and looking at its equipment. Discussing the net with its rigging, the strength of the winch, the diesel engine, gears, transmission and propeller.

"I really would appreciate the opportunity to captain this boat for you," Tony said. "I can handle her, and I'll treat her like my own."

I could see the sincerity in his eyes. "Why not," I said, "I can't run it by myself." So yes, yes Captain, when can we go drag? This was the start of a good friendship.

Slowly, I learned to trust and count on Captain Tony. Every day, at least twice or more, he was at the dock tinkering with the little boat, adjusting the gear and arranging the deck to improve the workflow and hopefully improve our shrimping chances. Knowing his way around a working shrimp boat, he made several improvements to the little shrimper. Tony believed in keeping the boat clean and all the equipment in good working order.

"The boat is ready, Boss Lady." That's what Tony called me – "Boss Lady." We both were ready to get the net wet. Now, we just needed to start dragging. Tony and I would obviously need some help working the boat, so he picked up Chad to be a deck hand.

Together they made a good duo. I liked Chad; he would bring me treasures found among the shrimp in the net. Whenever he discovered something extra or interesting inside the net other than shrimp, he would bag and bring it to me later. Never know what you're going to find as you drag these waters. With each tide comes new life. After big storms is the best time to find these treasures, items that have ridden the currents on the ocean's floor and come to rest again in these shallow waters where we drag. It was always exciting to see Chad headed toward me with a small bag. "What have you got there, Chad?" I would ask as he walked toward me. He had a pleasant smile, and I always knew he held a treasure from a drag. Tony would tell me, letting the cat out of the bag, so to speak, when Chad had a surprise for me. Tony would say, "Boss Lady," Chad's got something for you today. He'll be there soon to give it to you."

Thinking back, recalling these treasures, sea glass was a favorite of mine. The mystery of where it had traveled, how far it had tumbled to arrive in our waters and how long it had been on the ocean floor has always intrigued me. Sea glass is smooth and polished from rolling along the sandy bottom of the ocean. Even an actual shell, if he thought it was different somehow, he would toss it aside for me.

There had been an occasional piece of wood also preserved by the salt of the sea. Simple items given with true sincerity. He liked seeing me smile, and I liked his smile, as he gave me the treasures. I guess we were just some smiling people, from the sound of it all, happy-go-lucky, so to speak.

I can see Chad now as he would ride the back platform, holding onto a support beam with his bandanna wrapped around his head. Whenever I went out on a drag with these two, I always felt safe. Tony told me one time, after I inquired about the possibility of sinking,

"No, Boss Lady, we're not going to sink. If ever something were to happen, we would run her up on the bank."

That satisfied me, that he had a plan. I loved riding the boat with these two. It didn't seem like work at all, not to me. This was an unimaginable workday, the sea breeze blowing with the salt mist hitting your face, watching the seagulls fly and dive for the shrimp as they jumped up out of the water trying to avoid the net.

Watching the dolphins was my favorite, as we prepared to drag; you could see them coming from far in the distance. Tony said they recognized the sound of the diesel engines and could hear the rattle of the chains as we lowered the net.

The dolphins would swim along beside the boat waiting for their opportunity to catch their fill of fish as we pulled the net. They seemed to understand what we were doing and waited patiently.

One trip out, I recall having an issue with the winch. While making adjustments before lowering the net, we were just drifting and idling along. I looked over beside the boat and saw a dolphin's head raised up out of the water. He was close, close enough to see his eyes and knowing smile, as he watched our every move. At that moment the world stopped spinning, a true connection with nature. Realizing the obvious, we were both there for the same thing. It seemed as if he was asking, "What's taking so long?"

He watched and waited patiently as we got ready. I was

fascinated, wondering what thoughts were going through his mind. I think he understood. It was amazing witnessing the intelligence that these creatures possess. A partnership of sorts, fishing together, chasing these tides, searching for shrimp. Once the net was lowered, it was game on for both of us.

It was a completely different life for me. Nothing remotely close to my career in the medical field. Chad showed me how to cull shrimp on the back platform after pulling up the net. Throwing the little fish back was the most important thing for me, and I would do so before touching any of the shrimp. It seemed like the right thing to-do, get as many back into the water as possible before they died. Chad even showed me how to feed a dolphin with the fish that came up in the net. That was truly amazing. It was a great photo opportunity, and these opportunities were plentiful. Life there was very different for me but good; I felt great out on the water and eventually would have the best suntan of my life.

On dragging days, Tony and Chad would drag, filling the shrimp baskets to the brim and bring them to the seafood stand to sell. I had a roadside seafood stand in front of the Manor, which was my home along McCalleys Creek. Fresh shrimp would come in, we'd ice them down in coolers and then sell them to our customers. I loved the steady influx of people stopping by the stand, getting shrimp and eventually blue crab as well. I enjoyed conversations with each one of these customers. This was totally new to me – a tent salesman is what I had become. I had always dreamed of having a store and selling everything from pee pots to pianos. This was as close as I had ever come.

As traffic passed, an occasional horn would blow. One of my favorite customers, who just happened to be a South Carolina Law Enforcement Division Officer (SLED) in the area, would blow his car horn and say my name over the loudspeaker. "Terry, Terry, Terry," he would say as he traveled past the roadside stand. You know we were both smiling. I wouldn't even need to look up, just throw my hand up high.

He had purchased a boat from me, and we became good friends. It was a beautiful boat I bought down in Florida during the summer, a little twenty-foot black and white cabin cruiser with a 150 Yamaha. It suited him perfectly; it even looked like an officer's boat, real official like.

There were lots of people I would come to know as they became regular customers, stopping to see what we had at the stand. "Hey lady, what size shrimp did you get today?" they would ask. "I'll take a pound," was a regular request.

This was a whole new experience for me, something completely different than anything I had ever encountered. I was having the best time. It was great being outside in the sun, fresh air blowing in the breeze with a steady flow of people talking, joking and enjoying the day. Business was good. Unfortunately, Tony and Barbara, the seafood-stand attendant I had hired, didn't get along; they didn't see eye to eye so to speak. That made things tough. I like to get along with everyone. Being a true Libra with a easy-going nature, I like everything to go smoothly. I tried unsuccessfully to encourage a positive work environment. Eventually, this combination would cause a negative energy, and a dark cloud would form over the roadside stand and bring my tent salesman experience to an end and my seafood stand closed briefly. Shrimping continued with an adjustment or two but never seemed to be as fun for me.

The boat dock was a busy place as well – people going and coming with shrimp and other seafood, boats traveling in and out all during the day and throughout the night. My little day boat was much smaller and cost less to operate than the larger shrimpers in the area. Often, I was asked about selling her. "No, not yet," I would say.

My boat took a few blows while down at the dock, that was for sure. It was a long ride from the house, over to the island, where the dock was located. I would make that trip twice a day before Tony came along.

Tony didn't get along with an older man down at the dock. One day when Tony and Chad rode over to check the boat, they discovered a couple of men on board. The older man was standing on the pier pointing and instructing the men on the boat. From the parking lot they could see the engine cover was off, and the cabin door was open. As Chad ran ahead to get to the boat, Tony walked, dialing me up on the phone. "Boss lady," Tony said, "something is going on at the dock. I want you to hear this."

As Tony approached the boat, I could hear him say, "What are you doing on the Lady's boat?" Several times he asked, "Why are you on the Lady's boat?" Tony continued to ask.

The older man just stuttered, not really answering any of Tony's questions. Giving no answer for their intrusion on someone else's property. With the engine cover raised up and the cabin door open, it was clear they were up to no good. As words exchanged, I heard Tony say to Chad, "Throw me the line."

The old man said, "What you gonna do? The boat doesn't even run."

Tony put the engine cover down and then made his way to the cabin. Cranking the little boat up, Chad threw the dock line on the bow and Tony backed the boat out away from the dock. By now the older man was cursing up a storm. "Where are you going? You don't have anywhere to go?"

Tony said, "I'll show you. I'm taking the boat to the Lady's house."

Tony pulled the boat to the next dock, which was owned by his uncle. The older man was still walking down the dock, cussing. I wouldn't have believed all this, but I was hearing it all on the phone for myself. I was sitting with Barbara when the call came in; after putting the phone on speaker, she also heard the conversation.

Tony demonstrated to me later how he parked the boat at his family's pier and tied her off as he continued to be cussed out by the older man. Tony stood on the bow and gave the man the middle finger proudly. I was impressed by Tony's cool head throughout this heated event. Never once did I hear Tony curse, as he was being so brutally cursed. What a stressful moment. "Lordy-doo" was all I could muster. What in the world?

A plan to move the boat to the Manor was on our minds. Preparations and repairs would need to take place to get the dock and the docking area ready at the Manor. The previous owner of the Manor had given me a floating dock, so it had to be floated down the creek to get it to the Manor. *Miss Alma* stepped up for the challenge, my little fourteen-foot antique boat named after my momma. The floating dock was tied to the boat and down the creek they traveled toward the Manor. Wow! This tiny boat pulled the dock down the creek like a million-dollar tugboat. Little Fella, a man I had hired to move the shrimp boat from one dock to the next was riding on top with a long pushing pole. It was like watching the story of Huck Finn riding his raft down the creek in person. Of course, taking pictures was my job.

What amazing pictures they were! Once the floating dock was in place, it was time to gather the crew and make the long trip from the dock to the Manor.

The route in which the boat should travel was selected; the crew looked ahead at the forecast and made sure the weather would be favorable. Now, the timing of the tide would need to be at an acceptable water level to ensure safe travel through the creek. A couple of days later, up the creek, I could see the little shrimper coming closer. I was so excited, my Drag-in Wagon was coming home.

You could see the blue top, the support beams and the net with its riggings over the marsh, headed toward the Manor. What a beautiful moment, standing on the bank at the Manor, waiting and watching as Tony, Chad and Little Fella brought my shrimp boat down the creek. Getting her parked, tied off and plugged into the electrical system, ensuring the bilge pumps were powered and the daily ride to the other dock was over. The Little Drag-in Wagon now had a permanent residence with its own dock.

The daily routine continued as usual. Twice a day, I would check the water level on the boat, the power and position on the dock. It's a lot to keep up with, and the stress of it all is a bit much.

One day, we decided to put her on a trailer. I purchased a used triple-axle trailer, made a few adjustments to accommodate my Little Drag-in Wagon, and all preparations were complete. The trailer was hitched to the truck, backed down the ramp and lowered into the water. Readied and properly positioned onto the trailer, out of the water she came! Tony and I both felt such a tremendous relief once she was pulled up the ramp and onto dry land.

A huge burden was lifted off our shoulders. "It's beer time, Tony." We both grabbed a chair and drank a beer. Sitting looking at her on the trailer in my backyard at the Manor felt so much different but a lot easier.

Relaxing was possible again. Boats are stressful, and eventually the stress of shrimping seemed to take its toll on Tony. Fewer and fewer trips were made to drag. One reason or another would come up, with the result always being, no shrimp that day.

Occasionally, someone would stop by inquiring about an opportunity to captain the little boat, but I felt an obligation to Tony and our arrangements and wanted to give every opportunity for our shrimping activity to resume. After a while, the boat would sit on the trailer in the backyard with no plans to get back in the water. Eventually, I decided enough was enough and put my little shrimper up for sale – parking her by the front gate, along the brick fence on the property. However, she did not sell right away and would sit for several weeks awaiting her next captain and crew.

Tony and I remained close friends and he would often come by the Manor to check on me. Today, pleasant memories of our unforgettable journey together cross my mind.

Chapter 3

Empty Pots

Back home in North Carolina, a man's word is all you need to know, he has integrity and is trustworthy. See, I'm from the north of the south – a genuine southern girl from North Carolina.

While loading up my little fourteen-foot antique boat, *Miss Alma* (That's my classic boat which I named after my Momma), at the dock one day, I met a gentleman who said he was a crabber. I struck up a friendly conversation with him as I normally always do while getting her or any of my other boats situated while at the dock. During this random exchange of words between us, I spoke of fishing, shrimping and crabbing and the desire to crab these waters.

Obviously, my soon-to-be friend was an experienced crabber as he pulled up to the dock in his small, flat bottom, sixteen-foot aluminum boat with – you guessed it – crab pots strapped to the bow. Well, it didn't take long before this fellow, Curtis, was my new crabbing partner. My trusting old soul fell right into this arrangement, 100 percent.

Full steam ahead, no barred doors could hold me back. No need to check his background or to see whether the locals knew him. Nope, just an agreement between two new friends and off to another adventure.

We exchanged phone numbers and home addresses and wouldn't you know it, low and behold we were practically neighbors. We didn't live but a very short distance from one another, about five miles.

"How many pots you got, Lady?" Curtis asked.

"Well, I bought one hundred to begin with. I wanted to see how things go. I hear it's a tough way of life around here, so I bought a few to test the waters."

I selected olive-green wire for my crab pots and a florescent green floater after doing a little research online and talking with locals at the general hardware store. Seemed worthy enough of an investigation at the time. Let's face it, who is better to give pertinent information than the locals who have been dealing with these obstacles here for years?

Curtis and I came up with a plan between us, to get all these pots rigged up and ready to be placed in these muddy ditches. We discussed many different strategies to place all the pots in the water. "Can't just drop a hundred pots out there," Curtis said. "These crabbers around here will cut every one of them and leave us with nothing. We need to drop a few at the time, slowly, not to make a big splash or loud entrance; we need to be discreet. The less attention we get the better things will go as we enter this crabbing arena together."

Let me take you back to a time before me when crabbing in the Lowcountry was dangerously hostile. There were crab wars in these waters with local crabbers cutting each other's pot lines for miles. Pots were cut to the north from here to Charleston and to the south from here to Savannah, according to the SLED officer.

I was told they were holding guns on one another and shooting the bottom out of each other's boats and threatening to do serious harm to one another. These crabbers were sabotaging boats, their motors and anything else to harm or stop the other man from entering these waters and crabbing. How far would they go to run one another out of the water?

As I said before, lawless men, renegades, not conforming to rules and regulations. Plus, having no governing body capable of patrolling and enforcing these regulations or covering this massive amount of water, it was impossible to stop them. These modern-day pirates were willing, able and capable of doing just about anything to force their control of these waters.

See, my thought with everything in life is "Less stress is best." And this undertaking should be no different. So just like that, with our plan of preparation and strategy of dropping pots complete, our adventure began. What a ride through the marsh it would eventually prove to be.

Curtis got his brother Earl to help us with the sorting of the crabs once we got them out of the pots and into the boat. Together, the three of us made up our team. Early in the mornings I would get up, gather my gear and head over to Curtis's house to hook up to the crab boat. We parked the boat at his house because he lived closer to the boat ramp. Just made more sense to pull the boat the shortest possible distance.

Getting out on the water at the crack of dawn is exactly what we did. I usually took the bow of the boat, with a high-powered flashlight in hand, Curtis at the wheel, navigating us through the waters as we followed our crab line. Earl in his position at the back of the boat, ready to sort the crabs. This was our typical routine, and we would keep this schedule for several months.

My favorite time was in the morning as the sun began to rise. At sunrise the sun would peep through the clouds, creating the most beautiful colors. Between the floaters, which are the marker for the crab pot that they are tied to, was my opportunity to capture those amazing sunrise pictures. I kept my camera handy, strapped around my neck. I baited the traps; that was my position on the team. As Curtis pulled the boat up to a floater, he would grab the line with a hook pole, pulling it closer to him. He would then attach the line to the electric puller on the boat and pull the crab trap up out of the water with the motor. As the pot came up, Curtis would grab the pot, bring it inside the boat, open the cage and shake the crabs out into a basket. This basket with its crabs then would go to the back of the boat and be placed onto a sorting table to be sorted by Earl. I would then re-bate the pot with fresh fish, at least three, as Curtis had taught me.

We always loaded the pots with three fresh fish because that was enough to create a smell or odor in the water to attract the crabs. Now with the pot baited and the door closed, we would inspect the pot, return it to the water and move on to the next floater in the line. This was our routine, and it was repeated over and over. We had the routine down pat, each step coordinated smoothly, like a well-oiled machine. If anything held us up, it would usually be me, taking too many pictures or getting caught up watching some wildlife out in the marsh.

As we traveled our route from one creek to the next, it was like riding a roller coaster, winding and twisting with its many curves, through these muddy ditches. I rode up front, standing and holding onto the T-top rail. I loved the wind blowing through my hair as we rode along, no less than full throttle at times. The next photo moment would surely come, perhaps just around the next curve in this muddy water or along these muddy ditch banks. One thing was for sure, it most certainly would not disappoint.

One afternoon as we traveled along our daily route, we found ourselves being a little behind the tide, and we hit a sandbar. Several attempts to back off were made with no success. Luck was not on our side this time. There we would sit on a pile of sand, like seashells on the beach, waiting for the water to return and set us free. At times like this, one just as well get comfortable and relax or pull out a pole and start fishing. Remember, it's going to take some time before the water returns to a level high enough to float your boat.

By now the seafood stand had reopened and business was growing fast and was too busy for one person to manage, so I found myself helping more and more at the stand. This allowed Curtis and Earl to work the boat on their own, gathering the crabs and delivering them to our customers who had pre-ordered them and then bringing the rest to the stand. The more time they seemed to work alone, the fewer crabs seemed to find their way to me or the seafood stand.

Rumor in the street was my boat was in the water at least twice a day on most days, which was not typically done the days when I was aboard. I didn't respond to these rumors. Now, with my eyes open and paying close attention, I could see the crab business was definitely good for one or two of us, just not me. Realizing things were different between us now, I remained focused whenever we were together.

One day Curtis called asking me to help with the crab run the next day. As he told it, he didn't have anyone to help him with the boat, so he needed me to help. He seemed desperate and different somehow. Something was off.

I had an uneasy feeling come over me at that moment. My heart sank, so to speak, or skipped a beat, my stomach fluttered as if full of butterflies. I heard my inner voice saying, "No, no, don't do it!"

I reflected on another time in my life when I heard that same voice and felt that exact feeling. It was while getting a tank of gas to burn a large pile of trees which had fallen on my property years ago during a hurricane. As I pumped the gas at the gas station, I heard "Don't do it." As I drove home, I heard "Don't do it." As I poured the gas on the pile, I heard "Don't do it." As I struck the lighter, I still heard "Don't do it."

I couldn't get it to light easily. Don't worry, that is why I had two lighters handy. I was prepared! Determined to burn that pile, the voice still said, "Don't do it." God, I wish I had listened. As I reached for the second lighter the flame came out and the pile went up.

"Boom!" The sound was tremendously loud, and the explosion blew me across the yard, rolling and tumbling until I came to a stop. Up I jumped to see how badly I was hurt. Knowing I definitely must have been injured by that explosion, I quickly rubbed my hands over my head, face and down my arms to smother out any flames that might be burning.

As I did this, I rubbed the charred skin off my right arm. My arm was burned in the area where my skin was exposed, the area where my shirt sleeve was rolled up. I was hurt very badly but was alive.

I made my way to my mom's house, which was a half a mile away from me, down the road. My arm was burned from my hand to my elbow. No skin on the arm. It was the arm I had held the lighter with to start the fire. My mom, a retired registered nurse, drove me to the hospital and helped me go inside. So, I recognize that feeling and the seriousness of the voice deep inside telling me "No, don't do it."

This time I would listen. At that moment I could only imagine ...

I could imagine a struggle deep in the marsh, Curtis would hit me on the head and throw me overboard. Saying, "No one will find you back here, and if they do, there won't be anything left. The boat, motor and trailer with all the crab pots and equipment will be mine. Free and clear. Thanks, partner."

What a nightmare! My imagination was running wild. With this all going through my mind, I simply said, "No, I can't go; park the boat and take a break. Everyone deserves a day off."

My friend Samantha was riding with me and heard the phone call over the speaker in my truck. Discussing our thoughts and feelings at that moment, describing what I could only imagine. She also had an uneasy feeling about it all. She commented on his voice shaking and picked up on his stuttering, which was not a typical characteristic of his.

"Something is off," she said, and I strongly concurred. After thinking about it, we agreed it wasn't a good idea for me to go out with Curtis anymore. Being that far out in the marsh, it would be hard to find anyone if they were left out there for whatever reason. After all, there's a lot of water out there and fighting the pluff mud, which covers the bottom of all waterways in the Lowcountry alone would be a tremendous struggle. We agreed not going out on the waters with Curtis was in my best interest.

A couple days later, it was obvious I needed to take an unannounced visit to the dock as Curtis came in with our crabs. The day I went, I took Barbara, the seafood stand attendant, along with me. I also placed a call to Andy, a fishing buddy who knew of the situation, asking for backup if needed. Once at the dock, I struggled with my feelings of disappointment.

In the distance, I could see the boat coming up the creek. It stopped a few hundred yards out. I was not sure what they were doing, nor who was on board. I could see Curtis but didn't know the other person with him. They were too far out to see clearly. Finally, as they came in closer to the dock, I could see it was a female. Slowly, I walked down to the end of the pier, there I could see the boat was full of crabs. There must have been twenty bushels of crabs aboard. Hard to believe the difference this day had made on our crabbing luck.

"Dag, Curtis," I said "things sure picked up today!"

"Sure did," he said. "We got lucky."

As he pulled the boat up the ramp, he suggested I take all the crabs today. I suggested I take the boat as well, to get some much-needed repairs done. So, without any words exchanged, Curtis unhooked from the boat. I maneuvered my truck over and hitched up to the trailer and secured the boat. In total disbelief, we drove away just as Andy drove up.

"Can you believe how many bushels of crabs there are in the boat? Has he been doing this every day? How much money had he been making without sharing with me?"

The gossip was absolutely correct. I was so disappointed in Curtis. Needless to say, we were done – this arrangement was over.

Later that day, normal activity continued at the Manor and the seafood stand. I had left for a short period to gather supplies the stand needed. While away, Curtis dropped by and went up on the crab boat. Nobody thought anything of it at the time.

The next day I headed out to gather my pots which Curtis and I had been using while crabbing. I hired a young crabber named Roscoe to assist with retrieving the pots; he was also familiar with the creek where we crabbed. Roscoe had been crabbing in the Lowcountry with his father since he was a little boy, and he owned his own crabbing business now, providing for his family. We hooked up the boat, and off we went.

Once in the water, it didn't take us long to understand what Curtis was up to when he had come by the Manor the day before. The throttle was broken. We were unable to operate the forward gear and control the speed of the boat. Rascoe was an expert waterman and a highly trained boat mechanic. He rigged the throttle, and we continued with our mission. The boat would definitely need some serious repairs. By following the GPS, we could make the exact run Curtis had made the day before. We were lucky to get most of the pots back out of the water. After unloading the pots and parking the boat, they sat in the back yard for an extended amount of time, waiting for a new crabber.

Returning to normal activities and other daily routines, I was in hopes of putting all this behind me. However, the word on the street was Curtis had sworn to get revenge on me by sabotaging my boats. Curtis's exact words were, according to his cousin, "I'll take care of her." I knew this threat was real because it had come straight from Curtis's cousin, who I had met earlier in this arrangement. According to the cousin, I was a respectable lady, and he didn't want to see me hurt or harmed by Curtis in any way. Apparently, this wasn't unusual behavior for Curtis. However, the warning came a little too late. Curtis had already hit the crab boat and damaged my throttle. I immediately told Tony to be on the lookout on the dock, with the shrimp boat and its equipment. The next day the shrimp boat took a hit. The throttle was broken, and this would not be as easy to find and fix. This repair would also be more expensive. Tony was so angry; he took this personally.

This was a direct blow to his livelihood. When blows like this hit your pocket, it gets your attention. Curtis must have traveled up the creek to the dock during the night and sabotaged the little shrimper, just as he said he would. After several weeks, all parts were found and ordered. (Being an older model. it was more difficult to locate these parts.) Repairs were made, and the shrimp boat was in working order once again.

Rascoe ordered the necessary parts and made all repairs to the crab boat right there in the backyard. He then parked it neatly beside the crab pots. One thing was clear in my mind at this point, I would need to find a new crabber. I cannot emphasize enough how difficult a task this would prove to be. As I had come to realize by now, it's a tough group of fellas crabbing out there, so not many are willing to get out and even try. I thought about Tony crabbing, so I asked him. He said, "No way!" He wasn't interested. I was shocked; I didn't think he feared anyone.

Well, the boat would sit for a while until a new crabber was found. I knew sooner or later the right person would come along. It was just a matter of time.

Good times and bad times, but all memories, some of which shall take some time to fade. More than one lesson learned with this adventure, my friend. Nevertheless, it certainly was an adventure.

Chapter 4

Creekside Manor

Full moon may have been my favorite time of the month in the Lowcountry. The beauty of the moon, glowing over the water, was a pleasant treat and even breathtaking at times. As the water moved through the marsh, being pushed by the current, there was a rippling effect, a shimmer and a twinkle. The reflection of the moon seemed to dance across the marsh, creating a beam of light with a romantic glow. Usually with the full moon would come high tide, or at times the highest tide – the King Tide. Both would fill the creek with water to unusual proportions. With the water at these exceptionally high levels, anything in the marsh would float. I've seen everything from coolers to piers moving slowly across the marsh with the rise of the tide, wandering aimlessly through the grass, only to come to rest again in its pluff mud and perhaps be lost forever.

The creek and marsh behind the Manor provided a spectacular view anytime. Standing on the bank, one could see many species of waterfowl, turtles, an occasional dolphin and alligator. This property was amazing. The main house, the Manor, was grand. Back in the day, it must have been a real show place. Would I live to see its transformation back to its glory? That was certainly a question in my mind.

My dog Lilly and I would walk the grounds on a regular basis. The Manor was separated from the rest of the property by an amazing brick fence and a custom wrought-iron gate. The main entrance was lined with palm trees, and a few more had been scattered around the property. Along the brick fence, beautiful deep red crape myrtles had been planted.

The property also offered exceptional views of the local jets, which flew from the neighboring air station. The sound of freedom they say. Yes, this property offered ample opportunity to hear and see all the freedom you desired.

The Creekside Manor was "roaring" with the sound of freedom, that was for sure; not a day would go by that you weren't reminded. The roar of the jet engines could be heard for miles. The sound never bothered me.

I was fascinated, always trying to figure out from which direction they were coming. They're fast and you had to be ready to get a good look. Looking up, you could see the eyes of the pilots as they flew over the Manor. Daily flight patterns would bring the jets directly over the Manor; and if you were sitting on the deck, you could stare face-to-face with the brave officer flying the jet.

The Manor offered the best views of the air show performed by the Blue Angels. Almost every day provided a fabulous opportunity to get a grand picture of one of the fighter jets. Often as the jets came around, preparing to land, they would raise their shields, and the pilots could be seen even better. I was walking around on the grounds one day with my friend Samantha, and she got the attention of one of these pilots, and he tipped his wing for us as she waved. Samantha was over-the-moon happy. I was thrilled as well.

I never grew tired of their thunderous jet engines. The advantage of their presence and the views far outweighed any negatives. They had daily routines: morning runs around ten, evening runs around four and from time-to-time night maneuvers, as they are called. At least two types of jets flew out of the air base. During night maneuvers, helicopters could be seen flying extremely low over the marsh. These were the peaceful and pleasant characteristics of the property.

On the other hand, there were spirits and ghosts roaming over the grounds of the Manor. The Manor's property was very old, it dated back to the Civil War times when troops marched through the area during the Civil War. The Manor itself was originally located downtown and moved to this location many years ago. Much effort was put into remodeling, creating the structure you see today.

Ghosts and orbs had been seen on my security cameras in the house and throughout the property. When sitting in the den on any given day you could hear what sounded like a golf ball drop and roll across the floor. Several times after hearing these noises, I called my friend, Samantha, describing the noises and discussing what they could be. A few times this happened in the middle of the day. Samatha and her daughter were totally fascinated with these events and experiences of spiritual phenomena. She wasn't sure if I was the bravest human or the dumbest for continuing to live there. Already, there was enough going on out there; but battling the spirits as well, she thought was too much. I agreed!

Late at night is when I would usually hear footsteps echoing from the third floor. Voices, many different voices being heard at the same time, as if I was hearing an entire conversation. I would lie in bed too scared to move, desperately trying to unscramble the words but never really was able to make out what was being said. Thoughts ran through my mind – should I tell somebody? Would they believe me? I was already sleeping with two guns in my bed, a shotgun under the cover by my leg and a pistol under my pillow. Did I need to put a glass of holy water on the nightstand as well?

Outbursts of laughter and music could be heard. At times it sounded as if they were dancing. Were these spirits trapped in a reel, partying amongst friends, or at a glamorous ball in the midst of a waltz or a foxtrot?

The smell of breakfast cooking was even noticed a few times. It was one thing to hear things but to smell them as well. That was too much.

Perhaps that's carrying this ghost story a bit too far.

The third floor definitely was a happening place. Did the Manor hold a portal of passage for spirits to travel freely from one world to the next?

What was the history of the Manor and its grounds, I thought? Are these spirits here to conversate with me? To warn of dangers or run me off the property? Or were they here because they were not willing to leave this world where they once roamed and experienced life? Either way, I thought hopefully, with help and understanding, we can all live here together in peace.

Old *spirits* and *haunts* must be driven from this property, the grounds, its walls and waters. New blessings must be asked for and received. According to the locals, blue paint must be scattered throughout the Manor for protection, covering all doorways inside the house and more importantly, the exterior entrances along with all the posts down by the dock and the pier. Most importantly each boat must bear the color of protection as well. Were all these occurrences just plain bad luck or was something more sinister afoot. Perhaps the property was cursed by voodoo.

Over on the island was a medicine woman, a direct descendant of Dr. Bird, who was considered a local hero of sorts. A dear friend suggested I talk with her. The island is full of spiritual healers and voodoo practices, if you were to believe.

Something must change around here!

I requested my good friends Willow and Frank from the mountains of North Carolina come cleanse and bless these grounds. Frank's a retired engineer, he's very handy and definitely a benefit to have around. Willow, on the other hand, works in the medical field, and that's how I came to know them twenty-three years ago. I worked with Willow at a hospital where I was contracted as a travel magnetic resonance imaging (MRI) technologist. We have remained close friends all these years and visit each other often.

Immediately upon their arrival, my friend Willow said she sensed an unfriendly spirit and an unwelcoming presence over the grounds. As Willow walked over the estate, she recognized signs of sinister evil more than she was capable of cleansing. At one point as we walked along, my friend fell on the ground. I thought she must be clumsy, or perhaps getting older and becoming unsteady on her feet. I didn't put too much thought into her falling, at the time. I helped her up and we continued our walk. While walking along I shared what I knew to be true about the medicine woman and her reputation amongst the locals.

"Honey," she said, "We need the help of the lady from the island. The medicine woman must help us. Let's pay her a visit."

So, with my friend Samantha's help, we contacted her, and she agreed to meet with us. Upon arriving at her property, she covered us with smoke of some sort, splashed water on our foreheads and said a prayer and a blessing over us. Once we were free of any unwanted baggage, we were allowed to enter her property. I had never experienced anything quite like this before. I was a little skeptical and so was Samantha. Willow was born and raised in West Virginia, which has its own rich history in nontraditional cultures, beliefs, rituals and protections. So, she was not surprised or taken aback by the welcoming ceremony we experienced upon arriving.

We sat, and I shared my recent experiences in the Lowcountry, the unwelcoming treatment and downright bad luck that seemed to cloud over me and my boats. After sharing these experiences in detail and the feelings Willow felt as she walked around the estate and its grounds, the medicine woman understood the seriousness of the situation. During this conversation, Willow finally came clean about the fall she took while walking over the property. She continued to share how she had felt a sudden temperature drop, how a chill had come over her body and how she suddenly felt nauseated and sick. Finally, she described how she felt a force against her back as she fell to the ground. "I was pushed!" Willow explained.

"Shuug," I said, "why didn't you tell me? I had no idea you had experienced any of this."

Hearing all this, the medicine woman agreed she needed to come to the property. The timing couldn't have been better; she was able to come out that very evening. Wow, I was excited, and so were my friends. We were wondering what she might feel or discover once she arrived. All of this was totally new to me and Samantha.

We headed back home and waited anxiously for her to arrive. Finally, three hours later, the medicine woman arrived. She stepped out of her car, took a deep breath, walked up to the front of the car and placed a large cloth on the hood. Opening the cloth, we could see several of the items that were inside. She arranged the pieces just so and appeared to pray. While walking around the property, she found several chicken legs with claws still attached, in different places along the brick fence. She also found black rocks (which are not native to this area or region) that had been placed on all corners of the property. Several broken feathers also were noticed as she walked over the grounds.

None of these things would have caught my eye or made any impact on me if I had seen them previously. What did it all mean? The way she looked at us though, it was obvious to us it meant something to her.

After concluding her inspection of the grounds and the Manor, she paused to think pensively, or that was my take on her demeanor. Returning to her car hood and placing some items back on the cloth, she folded the cloth up and with her arms raised up in the air, said another prayer. Shortly after all this, she shared her thoughts of serious danger lying ahead.

"You have a serious problem here for sure. I must return

home and focus on the necessary steps and measures to take to help you, your estate and its grounds. I will be in touch. Till then, stay off the water and watch your back." She touched my shoulders and forehead with a white feather and said a prayer. "I will return."

As she left the property, Willow, Samantha and I looked at each other. "What in the world?" Samantha said she needed a beer, and I agreed.

"Yeah, absolutely," I said. We all need a drink. Willow knew more than she was willing to share, but she didn't, for fear of scaring us. But she couldn't scare us anymore than we already were. I didn't really know what to think or say.

Days later, the medicine lady returned bringing with her white quartz, a rock found in a different part of the country, which she placed at all corners of the property. "This is for a good energy border for the grounds," she explained. "This will offer and invite good energy."

Placing the quartz all around the property, on all corners and bends, then continuing along the entire footprint of the land, she explained its importance. I'm not sure how many she placed, but it was a large basketful.

She continued by sharing with me the ceremony she had conducted over the quartz and several other items she would be placing and leaving on the property. She walked all over the grounds, around and through the Manor, dropping what appeared to be water and saying a prayer. Over each doorway, she would pause and say an extra prayer. When it came to me, she had me raise my arms, and she blew smoke over my body and sprinkled the same water-like mixture on my forehead and threw it over my shoulders. Again, she touched my forehead and shoulders with the white feather and continued to outline my entire body. While outlining my body, she recited a prayer. After this prayer, she took out a necklace she had prepared at her home for me, a necklace she had spent many hours praying over and asking for protection for me. She placed the necklace around my neck, finished her ritual and closed the cloth which wrapped each item. "All this will help you, my friend. It's the best my elders can offer to protect you, invite positive energy and increase good vibration over you, your boats and property."

Before leaving this day, the medicine woman encouraged me to pray to my God, asking for His blessings and protection. Some problems only God can fix, my friends.

Chapter 5

Chatter in the Street

Chatter in the street, eight-million-dollar gossip. "She's rich, the new fishing lady is rich! She's got plenty of money."

This is the kind of foolishness that must have triggered the wave of unwanted activity over my property at the Manor. Where did they get this idea? This tale couldn't have been further from the truth.

Doors rattling late at night, incendiaries shot out over the cabin in the wee hours of the morning. (See, shortly after moving to the property, I was staying in my little cabin down by the boat ramp, which was on the Manor property).

That will surely get your attention. Your heart pounds at a different level when you're asleep and a boom goes off in the dead of night over your head.

"What the hell?" I thought. I grabbed the pistol I always kept close by me at all times, day and night, by now. I looked around constantly to see and know who or what was in my immediate area. Late one night, I was awakened by what I thought was the sound of a boat motor coming closer. I sat up, listening to hear and understand if I was truly hearing a boat. Being pitch black outside, usually nothing stirred out in the creek over the marsh that time of the night.

I grabbed a pair of shoes that I usually left sitting by the door. I was in shorty pajamas; that's my style, with pockets, always pockets. I got my shoes on quickly, pistol in hand and was peeping out of the windows. Yes, I was correct, it was a boat!

Bright lights flooded the outside of the cabin as well as the inside and they were getting closer and closer by the minute. Realizing it was three in the morning, shaking, I grabbed my phone, called my shrimp stand girl, Barbara, who had become a good friend, and told her what was happening. I was so very scared at this point; I also texted my good friend Samantha and told her what was going on as well. Now, their boat was in my ramp area on my property at the Manor. Lordy-doo, it was a boat full of men – seven to be exact!

I could see clearly from the lights on the porch of the cabin. It was indeed seven men in a boat who pulled up on my ramp just a few feet from the porch of my little cabin. Both women told me to hit the porch shooting. I bravely stepped out onto the porch in my pajamas, with my pistol drawn and ready to fire. I held it up, looking into the faces of all seven men. They looked back at me with no words spoken between us. I stood steady, focused and prepared to make a move if necessary. My friends were both telling me to fire the gun. I held back from shooting, shaking and scared.

I remembered what my daddy would say when I was younger. "No such thing as a warning shot, baby duck. Only fire when ready to shoot and never shoot unless you're ready to kill."

Taught to respect life, nature and guns. I attended hunter and gun safety classes and hunted along beside my

I held off from firing but continued holding the pistol in a position suitable to fire at will, if even the slightest thought crossed my mind. The boat shifted into reverse, slowly backing out of the ramp. Not a sound uttered from any of their mouths. No apology or gesture of a misunderstanding. I was not sure what was happening. I was confused. But one thing was clear to me; they were there to scare or harm me. This was not a game. This was the real thing. Oh, my goodness! What have I done to deserve this?

Thoughts went racing through my mind. My friends continued to advocate shooting. The boat eased down the creek toward the motel property, which was beside the Manor, and turned off the motor and lights. Both friends are still telling me to shoot. "Let them know you're not scared."

But truly I was. Scared enough the pantlegs of my shorty pajamas were shaking. My heart was pounding in my chest, enough to rattle my ribs, my hands trembling, and I was breathing fast. I truly was shaken up and fully alert at this point. Now, there was no way out of this creek except to come back by me. The Manor was located towards the end of the creek, so there was only one way in and one way out.

As I stood on the porch of the tiny cabin waiting to see what was going to happen next, my friend Barbara remained on the phone with me, and Samantha continued texting; both continued to advise me to shoot. I simply didn't know what to do. I was running on autopilot. Still, I didn't have a plan. Things were happening too fast to be able to plan.

I guess you never really know how you will react in a situation like this until it's really happening to you. Eventually, the boat started up, turned its lights on and headed back down the creek toward me. Not knowing anything else to do, I walked out to the dock, near the ramp where the creek naturally formed a point and was its narrowest. I stood bravely, pistol and flashlight still in hand, continued shaking and breathing heavily while standing my ground. My friend on the phone could hear the boat motor as it approached. They still thought I should shoot my gun.

As the men got closer, I could see all their faces. I put my light on them, and they put their light on me. I then turned my light to my pistol and stood there. They turned their lights off and we all looked at each other with no words spoken between us again. As they went by slowly, I continued to stand there with my pistol raised and still ready to fire if needed. I stood on the bank until the boat was no longer visible and the motor was out of hearing range.

After thinking about what had just taken place, I realized the men were there to do harm; otherwise, they would have apologized to me for coming up my ramp at that time of night and for the lights shining on and in my cabin. That night, I knew, would never be forgotten. Going back to sleep would not be in the cards either. I now knew sleeping in the cabin was no longer an option.

I made some quick renovations (sooner than I had expected) to the Manor, and I moved. This would get me higher off the ground in case I needed to defend myself again. I would have height as an advantage. I also stayed on high alert after this point. Always looked around and listened for anything out of the ordinary. Lights were installed over the property and sleeping with a gun or two became normal. Twice my pit bull terrier, Lilly, woke me in the middle of the night, letting me know there was unusual activity on the property. Tony, remember my shrimping captain came to help me secure the doors in a fashion that would require an intruder would need to completely remove the door to get inside. This helped me feel a little safer. Tony also encouraged me to remain inside the house, not to open the doors, or go outside no matter what I saw or heard. He said, "Unless the Manor is on fire, you and Lilly stay inside with your guns."

The barn door had been opened in the middle of the night; I knew someone must have been inside. What will it take for this to stop? With all the preparations in place I still couldn't protect *Miss Alma*, my little antique boat, from these looters. They somehow were able to maneuver their way up the creek and sink my little boat at my dock without being seen or heard. The boat motor cover was removed, and the bilge pump wires were cut at the battery terminals. Tony spotted the boat motor cover and was able to pull it up at low tide. According to the boat mechanic who restored the boat and motor after it had been sunk, "A motor cover doesn't come off when a boat sinks." His opinion was the cover had been removed by a person, and the bilge pump wires were cut as well. Sabotage was the only logical conclusion.

Finally, I had a security system installed at the Manor securing all doors and windows, and I made a mental plan of defense and escape if necessary. I had enough gunpower and ammunition stored upstairs to hold off any attacker long enough for the local authorities to arrive.

The local SLED officer and friend told me to be careful and keep my eyes and ears open. So now, with my senses heightened and my awareness level beyond normal, I was alert to any activity that seemed different or out of the ordinary. One night I was lying in bed awake and thinking, I heard a motorcycle coming down the road. It seemed to have a smaller motor than some bikes, so it had a more putter-like sound. I lay there, listening to the sound of its engine and plotting its location on the road in my mind as it traveled closer and closer. I heard it get to the area in front of the Manor and ease past just a little bit until finally getting to the turnaround. My subconscious alerted me, and in my heart, soul and mind I knew this rider was headed to the Manor and somehow would infect and poison the grounds.

I listened as it turned and made its way back towards my property. At the property's edge, I heard the motor shut off. This most definitely wasn't a normal occurrence. I grabbed my gun and went to the window.

I continued to watch out over the property for a good amount of time, but I never saw anything or anyone. Finally, the bike cranked up, and I heard the motor head down the road in the same direction as it had come. I checked the security cameras; they didn't pick up anything either. Who was that? What did they want? What did they do? That was the real question. Time would tell.

*For all that is done in secret will eventually be brought
into the open and everything that is concealed in darkness
will be brought to light and made known to all.*

Luke 8:17

Whatever they had done at that point, I couldn't tell. All I knew was the Manor wasn't on fire and everything appeared to be ok and most importantly, Lilly and I were safe. "The rest would take care of itself," as they say back home. So, in time, I do believe I discovered what they had done. Their actions and the events to follow would be revealed sooner or later.

Chapter 6

Tent Poles to Fishing Holes

The roadside stand was a very busy place. Barbara and I sold shrimp, blue crabs, boiled peanuts and watermelon. The blue crab we caught ourselves, and the other items offered for sale, we purchased from local businesses. Managing the stand and keeping everything iced down and clean was a job, but Barbara handled it well. It pays to have someone with experience under their belt working with you.

Having her around was definitely a benefit. We worked long hours, and after closing the stand some nights, we headed out for dinner before Barbara would head home.

When we did get a chance to take a break and relax, Barbara and I would hit the water, trying our luck at fishing. The boat of choice would be determined by the amount of relaxation time we required. My good friend Andy, otherwise known as "my bodyguard," would go along if we took the crab boat out. He was well known in the Lowcountry since he was born and raised there. He was quite an interesting character and an outstanding fisherman by his own right – a natural born fisher.

He could catch a fish out of a mud hole in the driveway.

It was amazing watching him work his magic. As he told it, he didn't go fishing, he went "catching." By casting a small shrimp net off the deck behind the Manor, we could gather various sizes of shrimp to use as bait and improve our odds with the larger fish. We typically caught small fish in the net, but live shrimp would be the best bait for the larger fish, whenever you could get them. This property supplied everything a water person needed: fish, shrimp, crab and several species of waterfowl.

Andy could come up with the most amazing fishing trips. It was like going out on a well-organized fishing charter. We would visit his honey holes, places he knew to increase our chances of success, and they never disappointed. These holes were productive; we actually caught fish from each one every time we dropped a fishing line.

Several trips were made landing huge fish, which would eventually cover the bottom of the boat, because often these fish were larger than the coolers we had on board. I thought Andy's fishing abilities were amazing, "awe-inspiring," but he never seemed to think anything of it. He was so accustomed to catching fish in this manner, he was oblivious to the amazement others would experience, especially me.

I recall going fishing most of my life and not even getting a bite, much less catching a boat full or at least several very large fish at the drop of a hat or on command, so to speak.

The three of us enjoyed these fishing trips, out on the water together relaxing and enjoying the sun. Andy was a mechanic and understood the workings of a boat motor. Capable of repairing them while out on the water, as he proved once with *Miss Alma* on one of our fishing trips.

After arriving at one of the regular holes where we planned to fish, we turned off the motor, broke out our rods and reels and began to fish. Not too much time passed before Andy received a phone call requesting his help back home. So, we packed up the rods and got situated on the boat. Andy attempted to crank the motor, but nothing happened. He lifted the cover, checked a few things out, shook a wire or two and attempted to start the motor again.

Luckily, it started, so away we went. On the way home, we passed a few of Andy's favorite holes. He couldn't help himself. A cast or two surely wouldn't hurt a thing, Andy explained. Grinning, I agreed, but I didn't let him stay too long.

On another occasion the crab boat was cutting up as Andy, Barbara and I traveled along on our way to one of the local bridges. That day, Barbara and I wanted to get a picture or two from underneath the bridge. Sitting and looking straight down the bridge you could see for the longest way, pillar after pillar. It seemed as if you were looking down the throat and into the belly of a whale. We took all the pictures we wanted.

On the way back to the dock, the motor started skipping. Andy took the cover off the motor and started going down his checklist to evaluate the situation. Since he was not sure what was wrong this time, Andy called the local mechanic, who was also my neighbor and who regularly worked on the boat if there was an issue. My mechanic made a few suggestions, and it wasn't long before we headed down the river again. Fishing off the crab boat wasn't ideal, but it was doable.

While out on another fishing trip, we found ourselves deep in the marsh, fishing a little too long, as the tide was going out. When the tide goes out, it leaves the marsh pretty dry and bare. If you were to get caught out in these areas too long, you would surely be waiting the six-hour turnaround time for the tide to return, so you would be able to go home.

That's exactly what happened to us. The marsh bugs

are not friendly, that's for sure. Fire and smoke are about the only line of defense you have against them, so we found ourselves burning our socks, trying to defend ourselves. We literally removed our shoes and burned our socks, using the smoke to ward off the marsh insects. Honestly and truly, I believe they would eat the meat right off your bones, leaving only a bony carcass in the bottom of the boat.

Barbara and I didn't get a chance to go on many of these trips, but we certainly enjoyed the ones we did. Great memories and good times that shall be tucked away, always available for reflection as needed.

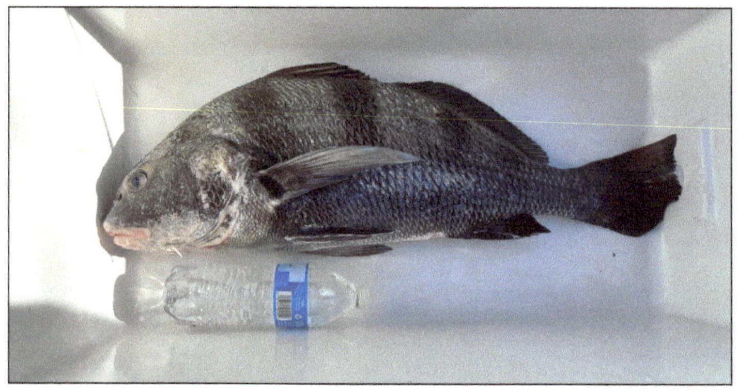

Chapter 7

"Sold!"

Lowcountry's Real-Estate Queen, they called her. Her office walls were lined with a multitude of plaques celebrating her many years of success. I had the good fortune to meet and get to know this fabulously famous lady. I met her one day while I was looking at a river-front condo property. I walked around the property, admiring its water view, and as I started to leave, a beautiful lady stepped out of the front door onto the porch. I asked her if she could tell me anything about the property as I could see it was for sale. "Sure," she said. "I'm the selling agent."

We never missed a beat. It was as if we had known each

other our entire lives. She had a strong personality, was well-spoken and commanded respect whenever entering a room, I grew to love her dearly. She adopted me, more or less; we were buddies. I was there alone with no family, in the Lowcountry or in the surrounding area. I moved there for a job at the local hospital. I moved in with her for a short time before finding a house and getting it financed. We grew to be close friends.

As we rode around looking at property, she would tell stories of her past – fascinating stories. She shared stories as far back as her childhood when there was tragedy in her family. She shared stories of businesses she had once started, grew and sold. She shared stories of her family and marriage. There was a particular joke she would tell often of the man she called her ex-husband. She would tell of meeting him and thinking he was a Greek God but soon would learn he was just a *blank-blank* Greek.

A local hero, a well-known boxer, was a good friend of hers. She would tell how she had hired him as a security guard or bouncer at her motel. She told how one night at the motel, a dance was going on and how the cash drawer at the door was his responsibility to watch. She continued to share how a hooligan had run up to the window, grabbed the cash drawer and ran off. Across the road he went. The security guard didn't follow him, but my friend did after discovering he had the cash drawer from the dance entrance fee. She burst through the door on a foot chase across the busy highway, over the ditch and into the woods. Fearless and brave, to say the least – a lady with a mission. Running for a while until the security guard was able to holler loud enough to get her attention and stop her. It's only $400; it's not the big cash drawer. That seemed to make a difference, she stopped chasing him. Returning to the motel, she asked the security guard, "What the hell, you're a boxer, the security guard and bouncer; why was I chasing him?"

We often laughed at that tale as we rode along talking about life. Often, we would pass another motel along our journey that she would tell me she built back in 1956.

A motel, "What's a motel?" the banker said to her as she was asking to borrow money one afternoon.

"I want to build a motel," she said to the banker.

"A motel? What's a motel?" he asked again.

"Give me a million dollars and I'll show you what a motel is!"

What a character. Story after story, my ears perked up, listening with total fascination. Having a strong personality and character, she was not easily pushed around by anyone, especially men. The good old boys at the local bank were no exception. My friend was on the board of directors and owned a fair share of stock in this particular bank. Not being invited to a stockholders' meeting one day angered her greatly. Who do they think they are? So, in a way all her own, she got even. She purchased controlling shares of the bank's stock and fired the board members. Well, this certainly angered them to no end, but she made her point. Eventually she sold the bank shares back to them, making a fortune. She definitely got the last laugh. The good old boys were no match for my friend – a force to be reckoned with for sure. The drive, motivation and courage she possessed, the characteristics of a real pioneer woman.

As we rode her buggy around the island, she would point out properties she had sold time and time again. There were a few properties she had sold three and four times. That was certainly a highlight for me, nothing better than jumping in her buggy and riding with her all around that beautiful paradise. I never turned down an opportunity to ride and explore with my friend. A smart, cleaver businesswoman with a great since of humor and a flair for telling stories.

"When you've been in this business for as long as I have, you can recognize property with potential," she shared. Also, identifying properties less likely to gain any value for resale comes with experience. I respected and held her in the highest regard. I didn't realize at the time that she was training me, teaching me and sharing her knowledge for my benefit.

One day while out riding around the island, we came upon an overgrown area, thick with brush and vines, large trees and a small ditch. Just a diamond in the rough, was my thought as I looked around. "I like this area," I said to my friend.

Looking deeper into the woods I saw a sign nailed to a tree. I was barely able to read anything on the sign other than the number. I shared my thoughts on the property's potential.

"Call it up," she said.

What did I have to lose? Would you know, a gentleman answered, and we discussed the property, and he gave me a very reasonable price. We bought it, and after a few months, sold it. Today, four homes are situated on the property.

Jokingly, her son described us as trouble, partners in crime. Shaking his head and laughing, he said that together we were too much, and he didn't know what to do with us. We were just good friends having fun. Three other properties were discovered and purchased and eventually sold during my stay in the area.

I grew to love and respect my friend dearly, as I have stated before and often. Persons of her stature are etched in the landscape and written in the history of the area in which they grace and live. She certainly was and is still an excellent representation of greatness for the area. More importantly, she is my friend.

Chapter 8

Girls, White Boots & Bibs

Three girls on a boat. You got to be kidding me. These girls, despite their look, were tough. Long hair, long nails, makeup and perfume. Always dressed to the nines. We had a bond between us – Ginger, Molly and myself, helping each other live out our dreams.

"Opportunity down the street," they said. "The lady at the motel needs a new crabber."

Several people stopped by inquiring about running the crab boat for me, but for one reason or another, I just declined any crabbing activity at that point. So, for the time being, the crab boat and all the crab pots were sitting in the backyard.

Ginger was visiting one afternoon, and as we tried our luck fishing off the dock in the backyard, crabbing came up in our conversation.

The short version of our talks, Ginger would continue the crab business, and she would be the new captain of the crab boat. Now, she needed a first mate, and she knew just the person. A great fisherman in her own right, Molly was a longtime friend of Ginger's. These women were tough, as I mentioned before. Tough as nails, and Ginger's nails certainly were tough, well groomed, long and custom painted. Most importantly, these women were smart and had a great work ethic.

They jumped right in – collecting crab pots, getting them back to the motel where we staged and prepared our crab pots, boats and equipment, cleaning them up and making repairs when needed. They scouted out new territory and set new crab lines. The local crabbers didn't make it easy on them. Even when I was discouraged and ready to quit, they asked me to continue and pressed on.

Women in a boat with white boots and bibs – your modern-day fishers. We thought we were fearless. I was their biggest fan. I admired their drive, courage and willingness to accept my wisdom through my trials and errors. They were problem solvers. If a problem came up, they solved it. They figured out how to maneuver these waters and situate their pots, even though the local crabbers continued to bully them. I shared with you before these local crabbers thought they owned these waters. They made that clear from day one. They were certainly not welcoming to women in a boat that were just as capable of doing the same job out on the water, catching crabs as they were. I loved going out on the water with these two women whenever I had a day off from the hospital. "What time is the tide rolling in tomorrow?" I asked Ginger.

She replied, "O-nine-hundred."

"I'll see you then. It's my day off, I would love to tag along."

Morning came. I met the girls at the motel where we parked the boat. When Ginger and Molly were ready, with boat loaded, coolers packed and new traps strapped to the bow, we headed to the dock.

"It's a little cool this morning girls, better tighten up those bibs," I said. Nothing like the cool breeze to wake you up. Perfect time to get Lisa, Molly's friend, to drop us off a little something at the bridge. I'll take hot chocolate. Never been a coffee drinker. Got to preserve my youthful looks. Can I say coffee ages you and brings on wrinkles? We don't want to do that, now, do we? The girls figured out what they wanted, so we called in the order. We'll meet you by the bridge. Should be there around 10:15 or so. Lisa didn't hold a public job, so timing didn't have to be precise. We pushed off away from the dock, headed for our first run, and after pulling a few traps, we could see crabs were moving nicely. Crabs were plentiful this morning. "It's going to be an excellent day, girls," I said.

Molly replied, "Great, I need a good haul. Got a few bills to pay this morning."

It was always good for everyone when the crabs were abundant. Nothing made us happier than a boat full of crabs. Blue crabs are a hot commodity in the Lowcountry. Those locals loved some blue crabs down there.

Pretty soon after pulling a few traps, we made our way to the bridge where the hot drinks were to be delivered. Couldn't ask for better service; good friends are hard to find. That was a hit – a little coffee and hot chocolate in the morning delivered to the bridge of your choice. A nice, pleasant smile on delivery; you couldn't ask for more. All right, off to work again. We've got to get out and get after them girls. We need to make the rest of the run; remember the tide waits for no one.

"Push us off, Ginger. Let's get to the next run and see if we can fill this boat up with some blue crabs."

Today, each pot was packed full, just like Christmas. We were excited! Never know exactly what you're going to get when you pull up a crab pot. Could be a surprise of just about anything.

"What have you got there, Ginger? Looks like a mighty strange crab," I said.

"I'm scared to look," said Ginger. "I don't know what it is."

It was an otter.

He had gotten trapped trying to wrestle himself up a free meal from one of our many crab pots. He was able to get in, but just like the crabs, he was unable to get back out. Being trapped and unable to get back up to the surface to breathe, he had drowned. Nothing to do now but get him out. That proved to be a little harder than one might think. How could he get in there? we asked each other. He's bigger than the hole. Shaking our heads, Molly and I got the poor fella out and put him back into the water. Ginger could not bear to look or even think about touching him. Our Ginger was a soft-spoken girly kind of girl, long black silky hair which extended to her waist, large dangling earrings, nicely groomed fingernails and makeup. Always dressed to the nines, not your typical crabber you see. We often teased her, saying she fit right in; you know, nothing typical about this adventure, nothing at all.

With the little animal out, we re-baited and inspected the trap, threw it back in the water and headed down the line to the next crab pot.

Each trip out, the girls ran into some kind of problem with the pots. Today in Willy's creek, we had twelve traps that someone had thrown into a pile, so of course, they were all tied up. "Total shit show," Molly said. "Took several hours to get them up."

"What the hell? I'm so tired of this bullshit," Ginger said.

The game warden says there is too much water to patrol everywhere. Seems to me just patrolling my pot area would be enough. So discouraging; grown men being childish bullies. Enough crabs out there for everyone to enjoy their fill. All it takes is desire and effort, just getting out there and trying. "Lazy men make no headway," as Papa would say. Got to get out there and get after it.

Well girls, just shake it off, clean the pots up and get them back in the water when you can. Dry pots on land do none of us any good.

The girls continued to pull pots that day, enjoying the sunshine, fresh air and all the wildlife the Lowcountry had to offer. Nothing like a day on water. They wrapped up the day with a few bushels of crabs, and everyone was thrilled. Back at the motel, business was good. Customers were buying crabs, laughing, telling jokes, talking about life and cooking up those crabs. Everyone has their own recipe for cooking these crabs for their families.

Two days later, the girls headed out again to make the regular run and pull pots.

Ginger called me up. "Well," she said, "guess what?

Hard to believe we lost another seventeen traps on the back side of Grasshopper Island this morning. They must have been cut last night or early this morning. Bet it was that no-good, low-down car salesman, Ted. We have seen his boat down by the bridge a few times this week."

Again, hard to believe grown men were afraid of women on the water. The girls gave it their all, accomplishing everything any other crabber in those waters had, as they willingly took on the challenges of the tides and battled the acts of sabotage from the local villains. Always in a clean boat with clean traps while living their dream and accomplishing their goals. I was so proud of them. Ginger had dreamed of crabbing for a long time; ever since I had known her, she wanted to crab. And now it was official – she was a real crabber with white boots, bibs and all, pulling the boat up and down the road, backing in and out of the ramps just as I had taught her, with Molly by her side. Both of these women had a great love for the water, just as I did. Together they made memories on these waters. Great memories! Memories none of us will forget.

Chapter 9

All Fish Belong in the Water

Freshwater fishing requires certain technique and skill. Big Pop, my mother's father, was a self-taught professional. "Hold your mouth right, keep your line tight and keep your eyes on your rod," he would instruct us as we fished along beside him. On Sunday afternoons, we would often visit his favorite fishing holes, enjoying this time together as a family, creating precious memories and learning some valuable life lessons. These lessons would remain with us throughout our lives.

My mom also had great fishing skills. She and her sisters had been raised fishing all their lives. On one Saturday afternoon, we took a trip to one of Big Pop's favorite fishing places, a beautiful area called Lake Mattamuskeet, which is located in Hyde County on a national wildlife refuge. Today the fish were biting really well. Coolers and poles lined the dock. Momma, Daddy, Big Pop, my aunt and I were busy reeling in the fish and filling our coolers. Roy and Tina, my brother and sister, had grown tired of fishing and decided to explore the shoreline. A rainstorm had just passed, causing most fishermen to head to their cars. This left the pier and grounds around the pier open for them to explore at their leisure.

Running down the shoreline, they came upon a few fish flopping around on the bank. Not knowing for sure what caused these fish to be out of the water, my little brother threw the biggest one back first – it was a big mouth bass, weighing approximately five pounds. Then, he reached for the smaller white perch. Just then, the most awful shrill or cry rang out, an ear-piercing sound sending chills down everyone's spine.

Car doors flew open, and people ran toward my siblings, fancy words flying around through the air. Some of the words we had heard before but others I believe were made up. Mad as hell is how I would describe the people's demeanor. Yep, they were mad as hell, we were sure of it. Scared us all half to death.

The fear of God appeared upon Tina and Roy's faces as an incredibly angry older couple approached them. Just before my brother and sister could be grabbed up to do only God knows what to them, our aunt arrived to defend them. Saved, just in the nick of time, you can bet your fishing boots.

Who knew the fish belonged to them? I understood why the fish needed to go back. My brother stepped up, doing the right thing, just in the nick of time, saving the fish. Being raised to respect wildlife and nature in general, Roy felt these fish shouldn't be wasted. So yes, with no one around, these fish had no owner, and while there was still time to save them, he threw them back. After all, they should have been in a cooler or at least in a bucket. Still to this day, when I see people fishing from the bank with a cane pole and a bucket, I recall this memory.

By this time, the family needed to go home. We had enough excitement for one day and perhaps had worn out our welcome. A great day with wonderful memories we still reflect upon now.

The next fishing trip the family would take would require a little more endurance. A rugged trip along the raging Roanoke River, camped out under the bridge all day and into the night. Campfire burning and yes, fish biting... big fish, really big fish, rockfish. Again, we filled our coolers, learned a trick or two about fishing rapid currents and played, as youngsters often do. I recall watching my Big Pop clean a large fish, season it up and place it on the grill. There was always plenty to eat and drink on these trips and plenty to learn about fishing and nature in general.

Big Pop was well known in his hometown for his fishing abilities. He was a tall man with broad shoulders and strong arms covered with sailor tattoos on both of his upper arms. I learned to roll a cigarette with him, a trick I found fascinating. Prince Albert brand tobacco was the tobacco of choice in his house. It came in a small red metal can with the tobacco packed loosely inside. I remember watching him place the cigarette paper out on the TV tray which he used to prepare his "smokes." He dispensed just the proper amount of tobacco onto the cigarette paper, rolled it up tightly and finally licked the edge of the paper. This helped hold the paper in place. Time to smoke now. Reaching for his *Zippo* lighter, which smelled so good to me; I watched his every move. He would roll a whole pack-full at the time and then put them in his shirt sleeve for safe keeping. Rolling up his shirt sleeve around the cigarette pack creating a boxed in look just above his sailor dog tattoo. Man, he was cool!

These lessons surely would come in handy somewhere in my life, right?

I would learn many other useful lessons from him over time. How to go out and gather black berries in the woods, then come back and make a pie was another favorite. Or perhaps, take the orange peels left from your orange you just ate and make an orange peel cake. As it turns out, these were all great lessons needed in this world of ours as we play this game of life.

The next family fishing trip we took was on a large fishing boat. Uncle Dizzy had a nice deep "V" fishing boat. It must have been at least thirty-foot long with a diesel engine. He took us out into the Albemarle Sound, and as we continued riding, I realized we were going out into the deeper water. After a while, I couldn't see the land. This must be where the really big fish are, I thought. After discussing this with Roy, he confirmed my suspicions. This was a nice boat, and we were all so proud to get to ride – a trip to remember, for sure!

I recall Roy having a large fish on the line and needing help reeling it in. So, helping him with all my might, we struggled for a while; but it was useless, and it ended with us finally giving up and turning the rod over to an adult. We were still too little, not strong enough to fight big fish of this size. Perhaps on the next adventure, we would land a great fish, earning bragging rights and practicing being big. Today, we had to turn this "trophy" over to the grown-ups before one of us or both went in the water or worse, lost the pole. Not sure why our sister wasn't on this trip because typically we all three went along with Daddy on all fishing and hunting trips. Tina was the biggest and probably would have been able to get the fish up and into the boat. This was a fantastic trip with plenty of fish caught by everyone, providing grand fish tales and unforgettable memories.

The most unbelievable trip Big Pop and his good friend and neighbor, the local game warden, made was a trip to Griffin's Quarter. This story would be told for many years in the little town where they lived. Here they would lose the truck, trailer, boat and motor. You have heard of boating fails, but this was the biggest failure on record.

"Did this just happen?" my Big Pop asked.

Once a truck starts rolling down a steep boat ramp, it's hard to stop. The Roanoke was a raging river with fast moving currents heavily embedded with large rocks and debris, dangerous on all levels. Fishing here was for the best-of-the-best boaters.

Surely, to be a game warden, training for handling the boat while out on the water and while loading the boat at the ramp was in the course. Sometimes, bad things just happen and sometimes everything just goes wrong. These men were certainly well-trained and very capable of handling themselves and their many boats in any circumstance.

Stranded in the dark now without transportation, they had to walk several miles to get out to the main road. My aunt, Big Ma and the game warden's wife were all worried to death. The two men were usually always back to the house early most evenings after a long day fishing. They fished together often, and usually, you could set your watch according to their actions. By now it was dark and raining, and everyone knew something was seriously wrong. The phones were ringing from one house to the other, everyone knew it was time to start looking for them.

This was long before the invention of cell phones. Down the long path in the wee hours of the morning, they finally appeared in the headlights. Stopping the car quickly, all doors flew open; and everyone hit the muddy path, running to meet the men. With tears in my Big Ma's eyes, she ran to hug Big Pop.

"Stanley, I was so scared. Are you ok?"

Both stood holding each other as the rain continued to fall. No one seemed to feel the rain or consider how wet they had become. The game warden and his wife stood consoling each other as well. My aunt, after hugging her father, went to get the car and help the cold, wet men get inside. On the way back home, the men would share their incredible story and the misfortune of losing all their fishing equipment, the boat, its motor, trailer and truck.

Looking at their wives, they asked, "Do we have insurance on any of it?"

Both these men were safe and at the end of the day, that was really all that mattered. All could be replaced in time, but the embarrassment and disbelief would remain with them for years.

To this day, nothing has ever been found. The truck, boat and trailer must have been caught up in the swift current and traveled along with the river out to the sound. Somewhere on the bottom of the ocean is an entire fishing rig worthy of fishing champions. In the lock box on the dash, you would probably find a box of Prince Albert Tobacco, Armour Star Potted Meat and some sardines.

This is where my love of water comes from. It's embedded deep in my roots; it's a part of my DNA. The desire to drop a line in the water and see what luck holds, it's called fishing.

Chapter 10

Motel Property

“Dang, Terry, there's an alligator in the pond. Have you seen him?” said the crab girls, Molly and Ginger.

“No, I've seen some red eyes from the cabin late at night up there but never anything in the daytime,” I said.

“Let's go, I want to see if we can get a glimpse of him,” Ginger said excitedly.

Molly said, “Captain Tony told me he had seen a swell or two in the creek and believed it to be the 'big boy' the locals talked about. A heavy, sixteen-foot monster, old and obviously very smart. They figured he'd been here hiding out for years on the motel property.”

The crab girls, as well as many others, found stories of the motel fascinating. They loved to walk over the grounds and listen to tales of its past. So, on this day we did just that, we walked the property, enjoyed the history and appreciated the views.

When I talked with the owner about purchasing the property, he told me to be careful because a big alligator was living there in the pond. I didn't even know the property had a pond. See, the motel was on several acres, all on the water, but it was grown-up with trees and brush; and even the buildings were not visible from the road.

One afternoon, I got brave enough to enter the woods just far enough to see part of the motel still standing. So excited, I called Samantha, and together we bravely ventured into the woods. Low and behold, after just a few feet inside the edge of the woods, we could see the old motel. Let's go!

There were three motel rooms and an office still intact. Standing strong with windows, doors and a solid roof, it was even dry inside. It was interesting walking through the motel, in and out of each room. In two of the rooms, we found an old Coca-Cola bottle opener mounted to the wall. We trampled through the motel and all over the grounds, right up to the edge of the water. Breathtaking views! What a beautiful site: the water, the marsh and the winding creek. How could this be true? I was able to buy this.

How could it have been lost in time like this? We couldn't believe what we were seeing.

Years ago, there had been a thriving motel located here. It had rooms in two locations on both sides of the property. The main building was a little larger than the other section. It had a lobby and living quarters for the manager. Each section had twelve rooms with an office and laundry area. There was a popular bar and restaurant located in the center of the property. A large pond separated one side of the motel from the bar. An inground cement pool and entertainment area with outside grills was attached to the main building. There was a circle drive on the property, providing access to all buildings, which made moving around very manageable.

The motel's well-planned, spacious footprint was beautifully landscaped. In front of the main building was a large three-section fountain, with water overflowing from the top and continuing to each section, creating a lovely entrance for the motel. Beyond the fountain, a large flashing fluorescent sign displayed the motel's name.

Today, the larger main portion of the motel remains intact, solid and dry. It houses the office, lobby, four bedrooms and the living quarters for the manager. The living quarters consisted of a living room, bedroom, bathroom and kitchenette area. The living room had a large picture window at the edge of the water overlooking the creek. Couldn't get any closer to the water, that was for sure. It was about five feet from the water. The inground cement pool had been filled with dirt years ago, leaving only the cement lap around the pool and outside grilling area.

As for the restaurant and bar, only the cement slab remained. Showing evidence of the bathrooms, coolers, septic tanks and parking barriers along the water's edge. The path circled the bar up to the water, then continued around the pond and over to the smaller portion of the motel. Definitely solid construction with quality materials, that was for certain. Doubtful anything would be built that strongly today.

The pond seemed to be a little smaller than its original design, holding less water and filled with debris, dead trees and limbs. Under several layers of dirt and grass you could dig, uncovering the circle drive with its cement curbing defining its borders.

Time had changed the surface and appearance of this grand historical site, but its memory would still be etched in the minds of all who had once found entertainment and joy upon these grounds. Often, customers visiting the roadside stand would share stories of the motel, which they had heard from their grandparents. The stories these walls could tell perhaps would entertain us all. Maybe these grounds still hold the spirits of these patrons which found refuge here. There were many memories created here from families resting during their travels to and from the Lowcountry, enjoying a swim in the pool, eating at the very popular restaurant, and others who may have enjoyed the bar and nightlife on the grounds.

My friend never ventured off too far from home without a cooler of beer packed. So, nothing to do at this point but open a beer or two while standing on this historical site and take it all in slowly.

Cheers to the old and to the new!

We were so happy to have found this, so we visited regularly, exploring all over the property. Laughing and enjoying the tales of the motel, its rich history with stories of good times experienced by the locals. The rumor on the street was that the motel had once been a brothel. It was a booming business, flourishing with a high volume of regular customers.

There were only two ways in and out of town and this was one. So, traffic was heavy both day and night. "Catch it going in and catch it going out of town," they said was the word, according to the locals. There were four turnarounds right there in front of the property. So, it was easy to get in or out, that was for sure. That's why the property was perfect for a business or selling just about anything – easy access. Location, location, location, as they say in the real estate world.

As we walked over the property, we finally found the pond I was told about. Slowly and carefully, we walked closer to the edge of the water. No alligators in the pond today, but we were constantly looking around, keeping our eyes open and ready to run if necessary. I could see now where the red eyes had been, which I had seen many times while standing on the porch of the tiny cabin by the boat ramp. No doubt it was where the alligator was laying, probably watching me as I was watching him.

So, I shared all this with the crabber girls, as we walked over to the pond. Everyone enjoyed hearing the fascinating stories of the motel as it was back in its glory days. Hearing the history firsthand from the locals was a highlight for me, no doubt it was always interesting. Also, understanding how it had been carved out of the woods, cleaned up and cleared to become the property it is today.

Often, the girls joked around dreaming of owning a piece of this beautiful property with a small cabin one day. Fishing and crabbing off the bank were the thoughts of most who enjoyed it here. A beautiful place, no doubt, with breathtaking views, while holding memories of the past and ready for making memories today.

Chapter 11

"Sioux Indian War Cat"

Checking the security cameras grew to become the norm for Lilly and me. One night while looking at recordings of motion on and around the property, I saw a fast-moving object. It appeared to be a large cat from the way its legs moved as it ran. After observing several recordings from the security camera, I could tell it was a cat, a very large bobcat, to be more precise. Never had I seen any type of animal like that here on the property. One time, I saw an opossum; and on another occasion, I saw an armadillo, but never anything like this cat. This worried me greatly as Lilly, my pit bull terrier dog, and I would go out each night walking the property before bed or even later, if she had a need.

I think she's some variety of pit, boxer, bird dog or cracker snatcher. I've had her since she was eight weeks old. So, staying close to the house with a pistol in hand and flashlight would now be the new routine. I started checking the cameras before going out as an extra step to ensure our safety.

One night, I was pleasantly surprised to see a little kitten on the camera, the prettiest little kitten I had even seen. A Siamese mix of sorts with white on its face painted up like an Indian with war paint and four white feet. I was so excited. At this point I had only seen her on the camera, but I kept my eyes open during the day hoping to find her. Upon a more thorough look at the footage, there were two kittens. The other kitten was gray with four white feet and similar markings on its face as well.

After telling my friend Samantha about the kittens, she decided to come and help me look for them.

"They must be litter mates," Samantha explained.

Probably the same daddy, since both had the same white markings. We were delighted! I never had a cat before, never even wanted one, but something inside me was drawn to this little furry being. I want to name her Sioux, Indian War Cat.

"Well, we'll trap and carry them to the veterinarian for a wellness check," Samantha said. "The vet will give them a physical, a bath and treat them for fleas, vaccinate against disease, spay or neuter and notch their ear."

The ear notch is to show they have been vaccinated and fixed. This is protocol for feral cats.

"I've got some traps," Samantha said. She was such a

dear friend, always there to help if I had any type of need. Just a good person, well-liked and loved by many in the area. I was lucky she was in my circle. We put the traps out and in no time at all, we had my Sioux. The cat and kitten adventure began.

I didn't catch the gray kitten right away, and she became pregnant and delivered kittens on the property. Several weeks went by as we continued to look and watch for the kittens with no success. Finally, one day out on the deck, I caught some motion out of the corner of my eye, turned to look and surprisingly, it was the kittens. Slowly they emerged, one, two, three, then four, five, six and finally numbers seven and eight came out. One was a bright orange calico. I never saw her again until she was about three months old. I have no idea how she hid so well.

So, eight kittens and two older cats joined me and Lilly there on the Estate. I took full ownership and loved them all. Often, they would leave the property for several days at a time, probably on a training mission, an opportunity for mom to teach some much-needed survival lessons. This would worry me to death until they were back at the Manor and eating twice a day again with me and Lilly. Once they were old enough, I captured each of them and took them to the vet as well. It took a minute, but I got it done.

Sioux remained my favorite; she held a special place in my heart. She was a true ham, loved to show off, rolling over and sliding on the deck to win Lilly's affections. She was top of her class and loaded with personality. When I decided to go back home to North Carolina, there was no question she would be headed north as well. Just how I would accomplish this mission, I wasn't sure.

Determined, I knew I would get it done. Finally, it was time to go home. The truck was loaded, and it was time to get Sioux.

Lilly was already in her place, sitting up front in her bed. I headed back upstairs to put feed down on the deck for the cats as usual. This was really the only chance I felt I had to catch her, everything had to go off smoothly. I prepared a can of tuna for this special occasion; I felt this would entice Sioux to come eat quickly. Surprisingly, Sioux walked straight in and right up to the feed bowl. I pulled the trap door and I had Sioux captured. I placed her in the carrier and loaded her up in the truck. She cried for hours on the trip north.

Finally, we made it to my mom's house, and I turned Sioux out in my room with a litter box (of which she was not accustomed). Lilly and I were happy to get settled. Slowly, Sioux would come to trust and love me. She and Lilly are the best of friends and are very close today.

Chapter 12

God Gave Me a Sandbar

The little shrimper parked by the front gate, with a "For Sale" sign stuck to her windshield was certainly getting some attention. Several   had stopped by to inquire about her equipment, engine type and size and of course – the price I was asking.

One young man stopped several times. On two different occasions, he had family members with him. "I really like your boat," he said. Not having the money to buy it, he proposed an arrangement to captain the boat and divide the operational cost between us or "on halves," as he called it. I hesitated, but without any other potential buyers at the moment, I agreed. This would prove to be one of those mistakes in my life I would look back on later and regret. The young man had a silver tongue, as they would say back home – clever, always saying exactly what you wanted to hear. Stunning sky-blue eyes and blonde hair. Very pleasant young man.

Later, a friend described him as being like a "used car salesman." We'll call this young man Ted. I didn't recognize the obvious in the beginning, but looking back, she was exactly correct.

"Saturday I'll come over, pull the net down, check the boat out and prepare to shrimp," Ted said.

"Great," I said, I was excited and looking forward to the Little Drag-in Wagon getting back in the water. I pulled her often because I had a 3500-diesel capable of pulling just about anything that could roll down the highway. I grew up driving tractors and pulling horse trailers, so towing a boat was second nature. I felt comfortable and confident.

I was once asked by a stranger at a gas station, "What do you pull with that fancy truck, young lady?" He obviously didn't know me very well, as you can tell.

"Anything. Anything I want to, Sir," I replied.

Both of us grinned from ear to ear and laughed loudly.

"Yes, I guess you can, young lady," the gentleman said. "I guess you can!"

After all the adjustments were made and the boat was organized and stocked, the crew felt we were prepared to drag. So, now it was official, we would drag the following Saturday.

Saturday came and we hit the water. The Drag-in Wagon was doing her part, pulling her thirty-five-foot net with ease.

She was certainly capable of pulling larger nets, but I had no interest in that. I felt this net was adequate; it just needed to be in the water.

There is a reason they call it fishing, as they say. It's true; there is no guarantee or promise you'll get your catch. Just time and effort, my friend. Do the time, hold your mouth right and pray, applying all your trained techniques in the hope the moon and tides will shine favorably upon you.

Several trips were made to drag, but not too many shrimp ever hit the deck. Not really sure this young man ever had a clue about shrimping. However, he appeared to try.

Loading the boat up one morning following a drag, we discovered something very strange. We noticed an area on the boat's hull that appeared to have been struck with a hammer. You could see the entire shape of the hammer's head as it had been pushed through the fiberglass hull. This would need to be repaired. With the shape of the hammer and its location along the edge of the boat, it appeared to be an act of sabotage. This had to be repaired, so I purchased the supplies, patched the hole and we made plans to drag again.

This time out, my sister Tina went along. I had talked up the shrimping experience and all the wonders of a day on the water with its spectacular views, sparking her interest. I was so happy she was able to go out and experience this with me. Shrimping was not in our family tree, you see. We were fishermen of a different type. This day, I would turn the picture taking over to her, and let's just say, she made me proud. The clicks on the camera sounded like an automatic machine gun.

If a camera could overheat and smoke from use, this one would be blazing. I joked with her, but I was thrilled she had been on board for at least one trip. We finished dragging, got the boat to the house, cleaned and packed the shrimp, freshened up and headed out for a steak dinner. Dragging again the next day was the plan. My sister decided not to go; I was disappointed for sure, but I understood she didn't feel well. Later, I would be relieved she was not on board....

Today was about to be a day I wouldn't forget easily. As we traveled along our normal drag area, the boat was slow to respond to turns and finally didn't steer at all. I've often said I'm lucky. Today, it wasn't luck – today it was all God! God had gone before me calming the waters and preparing my path. Today, me and the crew of three were saved by the grace of God. Looking back, I can see there was no other explanation.

My angels were very busy, to say the least. As I drove the boat, dragging the net, the crew members were standing in their positions on the back deck, ready to do their part as we attempted to bring in the net. This was the exciting part. We used the support bars to help us raise the net and swing it to the center of the platform, where we would open and dump the contents to actually see our catch.

We had been dragging for approximately two hours or

more, which was long enough, we felt – finally time to see what size shrimp and how many we caught with this drag. When bringing in the net, one should keep the net straight behind the boat, so the net doesn't get tangled. This is accomplished by steering the boat and watching the current as the winch pulls the net. Often, turning the boat is the only way to accomplish this since the current is strong at times. My struggle was increasing. I struggled to turn the wheel. The boat was not responding – it was not turning.

I yelled out to the crew, "It's not turning," who was yelling back at me, "Turn the wheel."

"Turn, the boat," Ted continued to shout.

The boat came to rest on a sandbar. Yes, a sandbar! Everything came to an abrupt stop.

"We're on a sand bar," one of the crew members announced loudly.

You know it was "the car salesman," Ted.

After checking the depth of the water, which was less than waist high, this particular crew member stepped out of the boat into the water, mad as hell and not understanding I was unable to turn the steering wheel. "Hard to talk to a fool that's not listening," I thought.

With the boat sitting on the sandbar, Ted was able to walk along the boat's edge to the back where the net was floating. He was able to gather the net, pulling it up with the winch as we normally would. While he was still in the water, I was able to communicate with him how I was unable to turn the wheel, and he finally understood.

While still at the back of the boat, Ted was able to investigate the propeller and see what was causing the steering problem. He reached over and touched the propeller, and it fell completely off the boat and came to rest on the bottom of the ocean. He struggled, pulling with all his might as he raised the propeller up out of the sand, off the ocean floor. A look of total horror – pure fright – the fear of God came upon his face as he held the propeller and shaft in his hands realizing this created a hole in the bottom of the boat and water was rushing inside. This wouldn't have been possible had we not been sitting on a sandbar. God gave me a sandbar! God and only God could have given me this sandbar!

God gave me a sandbar!

As Ted stood there in the water with the propeller held up high for us all to see. He yelled "What the hell are we gonna do now!?"

He then threw the propeller onto the back deck. Water was coming up into the boat through the hole where the shaft of the propeller would normally go as it traveled along towards the motor. Everyone was terrified; this was not your typical problem when out boating on the water. I was shocked, and I think the others were as well.

The oldest and most experienced crew member, Howard, took charge of the vessel at this point. He directed the youngest and smallest crew member, Barry, to jump down to the bottom of the boat, take off his t-shirt and stuff it in the hole to slow down the rapid influx of water. I jumped through the open windshield onto the front bow and waved down another boater as they were passing. Ted was still out on the sandbar in the water, which was still approximately waist deep, saying some words not heard in Sunday school. I asked, "Should I call for Tow-I-Can?" and Howard, the 'stand-in' captain said, "No, don't call anyone yet."

Now, remember the beacon is mounted on an interior wall of the boat's cabin. It's in times like this it would come in handy should the boat actually sink.

Standing on the bow of the boat, watching all these events unfold like a scene in a movie – a well-orchestrated performance, a real thriller, a natural water drama, a non-typical boating disaster, it hit me again. "God gave me a sandbar!" That thought continued to filter through my mind. "God gave me a sandbar!" There I was, on a sandbar, with all that water around me. Go figure.

The scene was set and rolling, a hole in the boat, sitting on a sandbar, taking on water, man overboard in chummed water, holding the propeller. The crew working diligently to slow the rapid influx of water and to summon a tow to shore.

How can this be explained in any other way? God placed me on the sandbar, where I was safe for the propeller to finally fall off. I wasn't sure what was about to happen at this point. The boater I flagged down had finally made his way over to us.

We threw him two ropes and tied to the end of these ropes was 'hope.' The boater tied both ropes to his bow and after several attempts, he pulled us off the sandbar. The boat was still taking on water, and Barry, the youngest crew member, was still holding the hole as best he could with everything he had available.

While he was down there under the back deck on the floor of the boat, he discovered the propeller had not fallen off on its own. It was definitely an act of sabotage. The bolts, nuts and washers were laying in the bottom of the boat. The propeller and the shaft would never have fallen off by themselves! They had been helped – a horrific boating accident just waiting to happen at any point. The Lowcountry villains had left their evidence behind. Not by chance, my friend; by the hand of man these events evolved and unfolded. You can't make this kind of stuff up, that's for sure!

By now, as we traveled along being towed by a friendly fellow boater, we had drawn quite the audience. It didn't hit me at the time, but typically there wouldn't be many people around when we went to load the boat.

Had my angels been among us, intertwined within the crowd? This thought hit me as being part of the path which had been prepared before me to recover my vessel and crew – with their hands and muscles lifting us from the water to the safety of dry land.

Getting her loaded on the trailer would prove to be the greatest challenge. Now that the propeller was gone, we wouldn't have any forward thrust to push her up on the trailer. Loading the boat by hand using only our bare strength would be difficult. Once we arrived at the boat ramp, several onlookers jumped in the water, offering their help getting the little shrimper loaded.

Wading in the water myself, pushing with all my strength just like everyone else, I wondered if we were going to make it. Realizing we were fighting father tide as it continued to go out, getting lower and lower and the boat continuing to take on water, getting heavier and heavier. We were running out of time!

Several attempts were made to push the boat around, lining her up with the trailer. With the tide going out and the current pushing the boat, this was more difficult than one might imagine. One thing was certain, the Drag-in Wagon was little in comparison to the other shrimpers in the area, but she was heavy.

Finally, we were able to get the boat up on the trailer. She was sitting a little off center, but it was the best we could do under the circumstances. With the boat more to one side than the other, most of the weight was shifted to that side. Having years of experience towing many different types of loads, I knew this shift in weight would cause an issue; and it did.

Now, with the boat loaded, I then took the opportunity to shake the hands and hug the necks of the many men who had taken the time to help us in our dire time of need. This was a huge undertaking, and we were so appreciative of their help. These gentlemen were truly lifesavers!

Slowly, with much caution, I towed the wounded boat and trailer toward home. The shift in weight caused the tires on that side to heat up, smoke and eventually blow. It was a long, slow ride back to the Manor, but I finally arrived on the bare rims, exhausted, relieved and thankful. God and my angels brought me home.

Everyone was worked up, wondering who would have done such a thing. A horrific act of sabotage. I wondered, "Did they try to kill us?" They certainly had intended for us to sink, that was clear in all our minds. Obviously, God had His hands on me, the crew and the vessel by placing us on that sandbar. If not, all of us would have been in the ocean, and surely the Little Drag-in Wagon would have sunk. If that had occurred, it would be anyone's guess what might have happened to me and the crew at that point.

Once I was able to put my shaking knees on solid ground, I did as my mother had told me – I prayed to my God, thanking Him for my survival and the survival of the crew. He placed me on that sandbar to show me what the modern-day pirates of the Lowcountry were capable of as they continued to try to drive me from these waters. My God saved me that day, and He continues to watch over me today. As I prayed, I remembered my sister Tina was home waiting for me. Thankfully, she was not on board for this event. I praised God, thanking Him; He had kept her home safe and sound. I didn't ask the others about praying, but I'm sure my dear friend Howard, the oldest, more experienced crew member who took over as captain, was praying. We are friends today and talk often. Many memories were made on these waters – good, bad; and some would be unforgettable.

Once I got the boat back to the Manor, she would sit in the backyard. While waiting for a new propeller, I took the time to find a new trailer, get it home and make preparations to get the boat loaded. Once the boat was on the new trailer, she would sit there, resting peacefully. This was a relief to me by that point.

Once again, all the repairs were made; and this time I moved her to the other side of the brick fence, out of the main yard to finally offer her up for sale. This time with no negotiations for payment, my shrimping adventure was complete. Been there, done that, got the sweatshirt. The smooth talker, Ted, on the other hand, was onto another idea. He thought he would take advantage of the crab boat and the crab pots sitting in the backyard. So, after smoothly talking his way into this arrangement, he took it out and started crabbing.

Buy this, buy that; and slowly, more and more would turn up missing. Slowly the silver-tongued devil's story would be the same as the other crabbers. No crabs today. Greed once again had struck in the Lowcountry. A cloud of dishonesty hovered over these muddy ditches once again.

All arrangements made between us were officially over. I was done with this young man. Taking my truck back from him concluded our dealings. Hard lessons learned, for sure. Less stress is best; and certainly less of "this joker" was more.

This troubled individual was a huge negative, with a dark energy and soul, leaving a black cloud along his path of destruction. Once he was removed from my life, peace would be restored, and joy renewed.

Chapter 13

Yard Sale

Praying one night as usual, I asked God, what should I do? "Not happy here in the Lowcountry anymore," I said. I had been away from my family too long. I felt like I was missing out on so much. My granddaughters and my great nephew were growing up fast, playing ball and having dance recitals. I was missing all this; and of course, my mom was getting older as well.

As I prayed, God asked, "Is there anything else you want to do down south?"

Answering, "No, not really." The answer came to me....

"Go home!" Clearly, spoken like an agreement between friends. Why didn't I think of that? That was exactly what I needed to do.

Laying there in bed the rest of the night, I was so excited and unable to sleep. I was thinking of the steps necessary to accomplish this feat. Once my mind was made up, going as quickly as possible was my next thought. I realized there would need to be a few things in place, such as a job and of course, housing. Wheels were turning in my mind, thoughts were racing. Getting all this worked out was easy once the answer to go home was clear.

Shortly after sunrise, I would make the first phone call to Margaret, a friend who had been helping me organize and arrange things at the Manor.

"Margaret, girl, we're switching gears. I'm leaving here. I would like your help selling and eliminating as much as possible. That will make the move much easier, having less stuff."

"Well, how fast are you talking?" Margaret asked.

"Ten days, I'm going in ten days," I said.

"Oh, wow! Well, no time to waste," Margaret said.

During our conversation, Margaret decided she would come out to the Manor that day and get started. I asked her to include the shrimp boat, crab boat and all the crab pots in the sale. She was shocked, but happy. Margaret knew the struggles of the fishing community here and my love of adventures; but she was able to feel the excitement which exuded from me as I expressed my desire to return home to my family.

Exploring with my daughter has always been a favorite pastime. Presious time spent together, riding around the family farm and through the woods on our four-wheeler when she was young. Buddy and Buddy-row, making wonderful memories together, one adventure after the other. Let's go exploring!

The next phone call was to my sister Tina, who worried constantly about me being in the Lowcountry. She was thrilled.

"Absolutely," she said, "I'm on board. I've been praying for you to make this move."

We were both excited, bouncing ideas off one another as we usually would when I wanted to do something in my life. I made one call after the other to my daughter, Lindsey, then my niece, Kristin and finally my mom. Letting them know things were changing and I would soon be back in North Carolina for ball games and dance events. I put my notice in at work that very morning. I also reached out to friends in the area, letting them know I was leaving.

One of my close friends just happened to be the pastor at a local church. We just recently became friends, but there was a strong bond between us. I certainly wanted to give her a call. She made and sold holiday baskets locally, and I enjoyed collecting as many baskets as possible to support her efforts.

I had a grand Easter collection, and I knew she would appreciate a few pieces for her church; and certainly, there would be several pieces that would make great baskets. I enjoyed talking with my friend, the pastor. One day, I suggested a sermon for her; she loved it. We talked about my thoughts of becoming a preacher and how this feeling had remained with me throughout my life since childhood. Often, I've been told I have a knack for storytelling, perhaps I should have tried my hand at telling the greatest story ever told.

Whoa, that thought takes me way back. All the way back to Vacation Bible School, when I was just a young teenager, and Star Wars first hit the big screen. That will surely tell you how old I am. That particular week, we had a wonderful youth speaker. He struck a chord, which resonated deep inside my being. His message and method by which he delivered it has remained with me my whole life. That week, as I read my Bible and soaked in the message, I remember being captivated by the words – the promise of salvation and the agreement between myself and God as He promised to go and prepare a place for me and for those of us who believe.

I thought this was "A BIG DEAL!" I remember it being so hard to get up out of my seat and take that first step towards the preacher to dedicate my life. I remember this as if it were yesterday, my legs shaking and crying like a baby when finally reaching the preacher. This was the week I would be baptized and officially made my agreement with God, accepting The Big Deal.

Being a collector of many things throughout my life, I had accumulated way too much. A huge relief of sorts came over me. The next ten days would be busy, but it would be a great ten days. Margaret took a day to pull out, sort and arrange items from the Manor and then started selling.

We had a yard sale – a *big* yard sale, a *really big* yard sale. You get the point. Friends and neighbors would stop by and add to their collections, and perhaps find a new treasure or two as they attended the great yard sale. Each day there would be new items as Margaret would continue to move pieces out of the Manor or from the bar, which was on the lower level, as well as items from several barns, which were located throughout the estate. Traffic was heavy along the highway in front of the property, so we had a good turnout for the entire selling period. This was a happy time for me. I couldn't wait to get home.

Everything fell into place so easily. God's hands were all in this effort. Within three days I had a job lined up with a start date, no less. God has always blessed me throughout my journeys, and there was no sign He was leaving me now.

All preparations went smoothly, and the day finally came to head north. Just as I had ridden into town with ideas of new adventures, I was now riding out with the same anticipation of my next new adventure. Not sure yet what that next adventure might be; but for now, I just wanted to spend precious time with my family.

The following morning, I woke up in North Carolina with "Joy on the horizon, a new day and a new beginning," as the preacher's wife would say. A woman of strong faith I grew to love and respect dearly. Each morning when she arrived for work, she would come by my desk and share this positive message for our day. Through her and her husband's many prayers, my laughter was restored.

Chapter 14

Hard to Be Me

I've often said, "It's hard to be me," but just being myself was actually the easiest thing I've ever done. Just be me. Mistakes, mishaps and regrets definitely, but wonderful adventures, good times and good fortunes, were in there as well. I've taken all the cards I've been dealt and traveled this road of life.

Life has its ups and downs just as the tide has its highs and lows. It has taken them all to create the me you see. I haven't lived my life from the sidelines, nor do I advise you to, my friend. I've always jumped right in and given my all – focusing my full attention, no matter what the adventure may have been at the time. Born to be a nomad, perhaps. Staying in one spot for life isn't in my makeup or chemistry. I've lived and offered to everyone my motto "Less stress is best." I'm not afraid to try a little something different, that's for sure.

Nobody has something you can't have.

I believe there's nothing anyone else has that you can't have as well. Hard work, dedication and commitment is all that's required. I shared this thought with my niece Kristin while out on a family outing many years ago; and it still comes up in conversation from time to time.

The last boat I purchased while on this fishing adventure was a twenty-five-foot center console Tidewater with autopilot. It had a 350-Yamaha "rocket" mounted on the back and equipped with more bells and whistles than I would ever be able to operate.

This boat could fly – it had wings.

Seventy miles per hour was as much as I could handle. You can believe things start to look a little different out on the water at that speed.

While out fishing off one of the South Carolina islands on an artificial reef one day approximately three miles offshore, everyone was laid back with rods in the water, music playing, soft breeze blowing and yes, sunshine – lots of sunshine. We had fished all day, and I guess we were getting tired. I was at the back of the boat with my foot laid over the rail and my friend up at the front of the boat with his foot laid over the rail as well.

All was quiet, everyone taking their turn hooking a fish and reeling it in. Nothing out of the ordinary until my friend at the front of the boat was reeling in her fish; and as it approached the edge of the boat, out of the water came a huge head with two big black eyes and huge white teeth. Its mouth was wide open, and the fish on the hook was inside the opening. I saw it all as clear as day.

It was as if everything was moving in slow motion. It was a shark! I still remember the water splashing as he broke through the surface, and its mouth opened. That got everyone's attention. You better believe both our feet came back over the rail and into the boat at that moment. It was like a picture I had seen on the cover of a *National Geographic* magazine. Wow, that changed the atmosphere a little! After collecting ourselves and calming down, we continued fishing.

When it came time to go home, we took our seats and activated the navigation system identifying the dock location; and this mighty vessel with its autopilot took us home. She didn't waste any time either with the 350-rocket mounted on the back, we plowed through the water, or perhaps just above the water, to be more accurate. Holding on was all I was doing as we skipped across the water's surface – barely skimming the white caps of each wave. This boat was made for fun and of course fishing. On occasion, the front bow would double as a dance floor for a good friend and I to practice our dance moves. Posing up front, on the bow like a mermaid on the front of an old Viking ship as we moved along slowly was a good memory. Good times, for sure and yes memories to reflect upon later in life.

I don't have all the answers, nor do I need them. Today, fishing from the bank while sitting on a bucket sounds great. I cast no judgment on these characters in this story or their roles as we played this game of life together. I just chose not to play with them anymore. Not wanting to hurt their feelings, I simply chose to continue my game of life on my own. I feel once you have wounded someone's pride, you have surely hurt something important.

A lady with a shrimp boat, really? Once a friend and coworker referred to me as being like *Forest Gump*, I took no offense. Not actually knowing how accurate she really was, we both laughed it off. After all, Forest came out on top, right?

Attitude and determination are everything; therefore, nothing can keep me down, nor should it you, my friend. You ask, "Am I fine?" Well, *you betcha*. I'm just fine.

These days, things move a little slower. When sitting at my scanner in the cold, dark, professional environment, I reach back in time to my memories: of the warm sunshine reflecting off the water onto my face, running with the tide and drifting through the marsh, sticking my toes in the sand and the pluff mud. I feel a sense of peace and accomplishment.

If there is a dream embedded deep down in your spirit, I would encourage you to go experience it on whatever level you are capable. Get in and get going. We're only here for a short time on this earth; so go live and experience all you want as you create your own catalog of good memories, which you shall carry with you when you leave this earth. It may cost you some money, and you may not be the best, but at least you will have lived to experience your dreams. If you find yourself drifting along with the current, may I suggest you drop the anchor and stay a while – you just might find a place you like.

Also, play often and play hard, my friend; and when out fishing, may I suggest you keep your line tight, hold your mouth right and carry a large cooler.

As I heard once, "It was what it was." So, with that said, that's all I've got right now. May the tide renew you as you play this game of life.

Until we tie horses again, my friend!

Acknowledgments

Thank you to the citizens of the Lowcountry who may have been in my path or presence during my time in the area. Thank you to my family for their continued support while practicing many hours reading this book. Thank you to my dearest niece Kristin for always being there for me through thick and thin. Thank you to my friends Calesa and Greg for offering advice and pushing me to express myself. Thank you, Patricia for helping to make this dream a reality. Without your support and continued encouragement this project would have been more difficult and no way as much fun. Your unwavering belief in me and in my words gave me the support I needed to push through difficult times. Watching you introduce me as a "Famous American Author" to strangers throughout our travels warmed my heart and fueled my dream of writing and storytelling. Thank you for being you and loving me. Thank you, Teresa (my lifelong neighbor) for reading my book and always supporting me in all my adventures. I am so grateful to have you in my life. Finally, a special thanks to my biggest love, my daughter, Lindsey, for continuing to believe in me.

About the Author

Terry Lynn Futrell was born and raised in a rural community in the northeast region of North Carolina. A daughter, sister, aunt, mother, great aunt and grandmother.

A medical professional holding an associate degree in Business Administration and Radiological Sciences with an Advanced Certificate of Registry in Magnetic Resonance Imaging.

Having a good sense of humor with a happy-go-lucky spirit, Terry is always ready for the next outing and good laugh. She enjoys boating, horses, motorcycles and firearms. She's a big supporter of all sports and the great outdoors in general.

Upon completion of this book, Terry was able to take the time for reflection and absorption of this adventure with all its experiences. She was able to process her emotions and analyze events.

Sharing these stories with you, the reader, helped her organize her feelings and clear her mind.

Terry added some humor because, frankly, that's her way. Her mention of God and faith in general was to reinforce her belief – He is real....

As she recalls these memories, a bright light ignites in her eyes, her heart pounds with adrenaline, pushing blood through her arteries and veins, reinforcing life.

Terry emphasizes her thoughts of time and the fact our time on this earth is limited.

This story didn't end with any negative thoughts, it was just time for the experience and adventure to be shared and put to rest.

Terry hopes that she's been successful in her delivery of this book with a story of encouragement for others to go live and experience dreams embedded in their hearts.

Go, see, do, live and pray.

If you've enjoyed this book, please leave a review on your favorite book website(s). Reviews are a great help for independent authors like Terry.

~ Thank you

QR code for Terry's website